Triumph.

Stories of Victories Great & Small

Featuring:

T.D. Allen • Ronda Beaman • Barbra Meri Frey
Karen Guzman • Jenna R. London •
William Lychack • James Magner •
Bill Mesce, Jr. • Colleen Kearney Rich •
Nancy Wick •

Edited by Meredith Maslich Eaton

Possibilities Publishing Company

ISBN: 978-1-947486-10-2

Published and distributed
by Possibilities Publishing Company

www.PossibilitiesPublishingCompany.com

Table of Contents

Editors' Note

The life of a small, independent publisher is one of endless victories — some great, most small. But each year in business, each title released, is a true triumph.

Possibilities Publishing Company marked our seventh year in business in September 2018, and this is our fourth anthology, which counts as a big victory because it's a hard time to be a small book publisher. There are literally thousands of new books published *per day*, and the fight to break through that mound of titles and find our readers gets harder every day.

And then each year it gets to be time to work on this anthology and I'm reminded of why we persist. Each day spent helping new and undiscovered voices be heard is a triumph. Each time a writer takes a chance of sharing their work with me, a stranger, is a triumph. Being able to put a collection of well written and captivating stories from new and emerging writers exploring the very idea of triumph is...well you get the idea.

I hope you enjoy our 2018 Anthology: *Triumph. Stories of Victories Great and Small*, and know that the fact that you are even reading this is a great victory for us all.

—Meredith Maslich Eaton, CEO
Possibilities Publishing Company

Introduction

Cathy Cruise

It's been said that the triumph can't be had without the struggle. I believe that's true, in the way that there's no dark without light, no good without bad, no pizza without kale. This anthology contains ten stories that prove the struggle is real, and the successes—however big or small—are as distinct as each writer's voice and style. They accomplish what I feel all good stories should— transport us, connect us, hopefully enlighten us, and allow us to fully immerse ourselves in situations that are at once familiar to, and wholly different from, our own experiences. I'm honored to have had a hand in selecting them.

What started four years ago as a collection of creative pieces that shined a spotlight on undiscovered authors has turned into an enhanced assortment of works drawn from ever higher quality submissions, broader viewpoints, and wider-ranging talents. This year we were gratified to name three top winners and seven honorable mentions from the outstanding short stories and essays we received.

In the first-place story "Hunger," we meet Arthur, a lost, lonely man who strives to satiate a ceaseless appetite. Against the backdrop of the beautiful and bleak winter shores of Cape Cod, we witness his aching need for companionship, his methods for sidestepping heartbreaking regret, and his attempts to reinvent himself.

"To the Farm," the second-place piece, introduces us to the unforgettably bitter, funny, and arresting Anna. An older widow full-up with memories, stories, and a no-nonsense attitude that can turn surprisingly soft, she travels back to the family farm to "shock the bejeezus out of whoever's left," revel in old times, and come to terms with her past.

And in "Waiting on Angels," the third-place story, we're put in the shoes of a reluctant caretaker to an ailing grandmother. As she tries to connect with her seemingly delusional relative, all while fearing something terrible will happen on her watch, we explore with her the roles of kindness and duty, and the grace of accepting what we don't fully understand.

Other tales included here also take us to unexpected places, unite us with vivid people and circumstances, and bring about genuinely moving moments of revelation. I hope you'll lose yourself in these worlds for a bit, bask in their skillful crafting, and celebrate their struggles as well as their victories—all while perhaps finding inspiration for your own achievements.

— Cathy Cruise
Author of A Hundred Weddings
Possibilities Publishing, December 2016

Experiences with Attraction

T.D. Allen

12:08:13

The thunderstorm slammed into town at eight minutes past noon. One second the skies were pale blue, thick with humid haze, and the next all went black. There was no time for preparation, no time to run for cover, to exit the pool, to close the windows. The thunder rolled as if it had been booming for hours, crashing so close together it felt like the epicenter of the storm was as wide as the state. The lightning flashed fast and quick, pulsating through the suddenly gathered, dense clouds, illuminating the ground in snippets as bright as flashbulbs aimed from heaven.

Lance R. was safely inside the Aquatic Center when the storm hit, and he was the first guard to blow two sharp blasts on his whistle. He was known as a model employee who never fell asleep in the guard chair, a hero who helped little girls retrieve their goggles from the deep end, a man with steady nerves in rescue situations. So why now, ushering an elderly patron out of the hot tub, did his hands shake? A particularly bold streak of lightning whizzed across the windows and Lance R. flinched. He actually flinched. He fought to get his mind on the situation: notices had been posted all summer about the faulty Automatic Lightning Prevention System (ALPS) and the absolute necessity of pool, hot tub, and sauna evacuation in the event of a thunderstorm. Lance R. was in charge of this evacuation maneuver and it was going to succeed. But when his focus should have been on clearing the deck, he kept thinking of her. It was like his mind had been zapped clean, his focus replace with an unshakeable vision of his old flame, recently divorced and moved back to town.

A woman in a flowered swim cap slipped on the floor at his feet. Lance R. cursed himself and helped the limping lady to her locker room. She complained endlessly about the closure and he gently pointed to the signs he had posted around the Center two months ago. The signs proclaiming the lightning prevention system was faulty and in the event of an emergency — like this one — the Aquatic Center would be immediately evacuated. Lance R. had studied lightning strikes as part of his training and he had half a mind to explain to her *why* lightning and water were so dangerous. (But he knew none of the patrons cared to learn that a lightning strike is nature's way of neutralizing a highly charged area. No one wanted to hear that the fifty-meter by twenty-five yard swimming pool had become a vast, ideal, positively charged area that could attract a mass of negatively charged ions from any of the thunderclouds raging about the Center. No one wanted to learn that the wires running through the massive globe lights dangling from the ceiling had become ideal conductors. Above all else, no one wanted to hear that Lance R. was due to install this new system — a high-tech static ion dissipator system from a Fresno-based specialty company — tomorrow.)

Finally the last swimmer had departed the building and Lance R. took a final sweep around the building. He picked up forgotten kickboards and dragged discarded power washing equipment back to the pump room, parking everything next to a massive shining box that was the new system.

But what Lance R. forgot to remove were two thirty-seven-and-a-half pound (dry weight) electronic touch pads. Black-and-yellow, they each stretched five feet wide, plumbing the pool's eight foot depth down twenty-two inches and hung in the middle of lanes three and four. With the next staccato burst of lightning, one errant bolt blasted into the steel and glass roof of the swimming pool. Had the new static ion dissipator system been in place, the bolt would have been repelled from the roof (or perhaps it never would have been attracted in the first place). But as it was the ions sizzled across the main support beam of the roof and found the one crack leading straight down a loose-hanging electrical wire, dangling from one of the ceiling globe lights. The wire fairly burst with life, electrified, wild with energy and flew this way and that, touching the ceiling in patches, attracted and repulsed, zipping to the side wall of the facility. Then another battery of lightning flashed through the sky, another bolt zipped down the pathway already established and crackled with such verve that it sprang from the end of the dangling wire and connected with the water.

(Perfectly pure water is a poor conductor of electricity. But impure water — such as swimming pool water treated with bromine, floating with sweat and detritus from humans — contains mineral impurities that act as ions and the conductivity of water increases.)

The bolt of lightning hit the water, and the water ions had enough conductivity to carry the electricity to the internal metal center of the lane line lying straight between lanes three and four. The energy surged along this pathway directly into the two remaining touch pads, still connected by wires and cords to the ten-foot by ten-foot digital display panel on the wall. It had been methodically counting up the time from 00:00:00 to 60:00:00 minutes, seconds, tenths, and hundredths of seconds, resetting itself to zero and then counting up again, over and over, day and night, until the electricity went out. When the lightning hit the touch pads, the display panel sprang to life, its every pixel bright bold yellow like a Rothko painting. Then as if gasping for life, it went black, flashed 00:00:00, went black, flashed 00:00:00, over and over again until finally, as if sensing its own imminent demise, flashed two words which persisted until the facility opened again and the system could be restarted. The words UNSUPPORTED PERSONALITY hung curiously alongside the college championship pennants and record boards.

The head lifeguard missed this display of pyrotechnics.

The receptionist did, too.

Lance R. even missed it.

No one, in fact, was an eye-witness to this lightning strike.

A handful of people, however, were witnesses to its after-effects, but due to the odd nature of their experiences with attraction, none discussed what happened with each other. They absorbed something from the lightning, a change in behavior, an internal illumination. But about how these changes occurred they never spoke.

In fact, the only person who finally understood in totality what awesome power this lightning strike held was Lance R. The day following the storm the Fresno company was unable to install the system – a storm-related airport closure canceled all flights. Lance R. made a case to the head guard and with all the patron complaints about the pool closure, the guard had to agree. Lance R. had to uninstall the faulty lightning system and install the new, but he also had to reset the digital display panel. In doing so, Lance R. found the panel had become a video and voice recording of everything that occurred in lanes three and four from the time when the center reopened yesterday afternoon to his arrival this morning. To Lance, the findings were quite startling, so startling in fact that Lance R. changed into swim trunks, dove in, and tested lane three himself. He swam alongside a matronly woman in her later years, quite similar in appearance to his own mother.

What follows is the summary of the video and voice recording from the display panel, which, along with his report on the Aquatic Center Installation, Lance dutifully submitted to the head guard and the Fresno ALPS company before packing for Auckland.

13:02:14

After the storm, after the center reopened, the first swimmers to enter
lanes three and four were a middle-aged mother and her three teenage boys.
She ordered them into lane three with an impassioned speech about how
downtrodden and brow-beaten she was driving them all over the state for their
soccer games, lacrosse matches, and swim meets. The least they could do was
swim on their own while she swam for thirty minutes on her own, probably for
the first time in ten years.

She moistened one finger, swiped the inside of each goggle, and squeezed the
goggles onto her crow-lined eyes. She dove in and took a few effortless strokes of
freestyle. With each stroke she felt her stress and tension fading, she relished the
freedom of movement in the water.

Her sons stood in awe of their mother. But just for a moment. Then the
youngest knocked the oldest in and the middle dove over the others, goading
them to race him across the pool. The three took off in a fury, stroking fast,
kicking each other, smacking each with hands and feet.

Their mother, having flip-turned and now swimming back, swallowed a white
wash of wake from her sons and immediately reached under the lane line. She
grabbed her youngest son's speedo, which arrested his motion instantly. "Behave,"
she said, shook her finger at him, and swam off.

He sank under water and felt the cool stillness below surround him, intending
to grab his brothers' legs as a gag. But then he heard it: his mother's voice. He
turned his head so fast all he could see were the bubbles of his fast exhalation.
The bubbles floated up the surface and his view cleared. His mother was a good
ten yards away from him, swimming freestyle with her head in the water, kicking
strongly. But even so he heard her voice. She said, "God help me. Some days I
just want to be alone. Even leave Jim and the kids. Just take off. Why can't they
just swim without all that horsing around? Why don't they listen to me?" The boy
surfaced for a breath and his mother's voice disappeared. His brothers had flipped
at the far end and were even with him in the lane now. They grabbed his waist
and again he went under, the three brothers wrestling hard like water polo players
diving for a ball. And there it was again, their mother's voice. All three brothers
heard it now. She was swimming breaststroke on this lap, her arms curved
inwards as if she was scooping water out of a bowl, her head bobbing in and out
of the water rhythmically. Her lips opened and shut to take small breaths, but

that was all. But still they heard her voice: "why don't . . . to me . . . good boys . . .
breaking . . . heart . . . what have I . . . wrong . . . leave . . . yes, leave . . . just swim
. . . just swim."

At the end of thirty minutes the mother had finished her entire workout,
had time for a three hundred cool-down and still her sons were circle
swimming one behind the other as if their coach were standing over their lane
barking directions. She marveled at their behavior and wondered what, for
once, she had done right.

(Each brother could tell the other had heard something; they could tell when
the eldest brother fixed the parents bacon and eggs on a Sunday, the middle
brother consistently practiced the piano without being threatened anymore, and
the youngest began hugging and kissing his mother good night, every night.
There was a closeness that had not been present before, an invisible tie each to
their mother now strong and pure. Their mother did not know what caused her
son's behavior to improve and she found herself laughing, something she realized
she had long ago forgotten to do.)

52:13:08

Lanes three and four were empty for a long while before a young mother
and father and their six-month-old baby arrived. The mother used to be a
competitive swimmer herself, but the father had been a track star. He was as
comfortable in the water as a rock: all sink, no float.

The baby was indifferent.

The mother cooed to her child and talked in soothing tones about how
wonderful the water would feel on his arms, how nice it would be to kick his legs
freely through the cool blueness. The baby smiled and clapped at anything his
mother said, and looked curiously about when his mother set him into a small,
blue plastic floating ring. The mother jumped into lane three and treaded water
while the father nervously handed the baby in the ring down. He left the care
of the baby entirely to his wife; he was uncomfortable around children, afraid
he would break them somehow accidentally. He paced the deck and shouted
agitatedly at his wife, "Keep his head up! Keep your hands on his belly! That's far
enough!" His wife just laughed and called him a wimp. "Don't be scared of a little
H2O," she said. "Jump in and swim."

The father turned his back on his wife and child, upset at this goading. But
then he could hear his wife's laughter and his baby's happiness. So he half-dove,

half-jumped into lane four — a perfect ten belly flop — and swam like Tarzan, chest and shoulders out of the water, legs kicking furiously, until he reached his wife. "That's enough," the father panted. "Let's go back."

"But he's happy," the mother said. The baby splashed his arms and his legs were a mini torrent, soft foamy white water spraying into the air. "I think he's going to be a butterflier," the mother said proudly. She slipped the baby out of the floating ring and treaded water while guiding him by the stomach across the pool. The father held the lane line, panicking. "Don't let go! "

"See?" the mother shouted across the lane line. "He'll even be fine under water." And she gently sang "Five Little Ducks" and swam her son around in a circle. When she sang "over the hills" she dipped her baby under the surface – just briefly – and he came back into the air, eyes bright, mouth wide with wonder.

The father protested. "That cannot be good for him at this age, going underwater," he said.

"The American Academy of Pediatrics says it's fine. Healthy, even, to learn how to swim early," the mother said. "Go under with him, he'll like that."

The father grumbled. But with the lane line between them and his wife and child floating together like an island in the middle of the pool, what could he do? So he went under, expecting to see a register of fear on his son's face, expecting to reach across and somehow save him. The father did not expect to hear anything. But he did. His son, of course, was too young to speak, but was a fully conscious, sentient human being. The father dipped under the surface every time his son dipped under and he heard no *specific* words. But he heard sounds that distinctly *he* made, he heard his voice and the way he was beginning to speak: that giggle he made when he first woke up in the mornings, that 'ad-da-da' sound the father hoped meant 'Daddy,' that sweet, soprano squeak he made whenever he sneezed or whenever their dog scratched himself. Something changed in the father underwater with his son, a tightening that had been around his chest, a constriction of feeling and emotion, a sense that all closeness should be repelled, left his body.

The father floated effortlessly for the first time in his life.

18:13:20

The next swimmers in lanes three and four were a young Civil Engineering PhD candidate from Pakistan (three) and a middle-aged professor of Gerontology from Switzerland (four). They were strangers to each other, to each other's languages and professions, but both women enjoyed swimming for similar reasons: lap after lap, stroke after stroke, their bodies moved almost automatically without thought, and their minds became free-associative brain-powers, solving complicated academic problems before they exited the pool. The Pakistani woman was particularly concerned about her dissertation research (*Probabilistic Calculations of Soil Models*) and before she reached the opposite wall, her mind was already racing through the possible flaws with her latest model. The Swiss woman was writing a grant to research *Supercentenarians in Africa* and was having a mental block about the her proposed possible findings. Rather than slicing through the water as cleanly as a knife like she usually did, she dove awkwardly, creating a large splash and wave that careened over the lane line into lane three.

Even though the Synchronized Swimming Team was not practicing, the Pakistani woman became convinced their underwater sound system must be on the fritz: she heard blasts of rapid French, German, and English across the lane line. At first it interrupted her thought process, but then it became a melodic mantra, and she found herself swimming longer than she had intended. The Swiss woman, too, swam faster and harder and wondered what music the lifeguards were playing. They were both too consumed by their academic problems— and amazed at how easily they reached solutions — to realize answers they found came from underneath the water itself.

00:00:13

As the day grew long, fewer and fewer swimmers entered the pool until the Masters swim team arrived for their regular six o'clock practice. There was an open water swim across the Chesapeake Bay at the weekend and many team swimmers took the night off, tapering, so attendance was light.

Normally lanes three and four would be crowded with up to eight swimmers each, the fastest groups on the team. But tonight he stood alone at lane four, she at lane three. The coach barked out the warm-up — 5-4-3-2-1 — and he adjusted his goggles, preparing to dive. She waited patiently for the coach to come over with his white board and show her the warm-up written out: 500 swim, 400 kick, 300 pull, 200 IM, and 100 scull. She nodded, smiled, put hand to lip to gesture "thank you."

He dove in, thinking about that woman in lane three. He had noticed her months ago, how she was beautiful, lean, and strong, but seemed shy. Or was that her deafness? Perhaps it was her lack of spoken language that made her appear shy, but in reality, in sign language she was really loquacious. He had often thought about asking her out, for coffee or to a movie (could they watch a movie together? Which theaters had subtitles?), but by the time warm-ups were done he was usually so focused on the next set and the next and the next and then practice was done and the guys were showering up and talking about their weekends, he just forgot about her until standing on deck, waiting for warm-ups before the next practice.

He pulled with his right arm, tucked his head to chest, and flipped his legs over, landing with his feet squarely pressed into the touchpad. She flipped, too, at the exact same moment, and then they pushed off the wall, parallel torpedoes shooting straight in perfect streamline position. Their bubbles from exhaled breaths rose to the surface, mingling together across the lane line.

She tried to concentrate on her own stroke, on breathing every fifth so she could alternate breathing left-right-left. She had a tendency to do everything with her left side: breathe on the left, flip with her left hand outstretched, and she knew this was causing a tightening on her right side that was throwing her stroke off-balance. He began to pull away from her and now she was watching the wake from his feet, from his natural ten-beat kick and she longed to be that strong and fast. She had watched him often, hanging onto the wall with her teammates while reading the next set the coach had scribbled out. He seemed kindly, helping other swimmers in his lane with stroke technique, checking on teammates with pulled muscles. She caught his eye from time to time, but then he'd look away, down at his hands as if he did not understand how they worked in her language.

She was entering the flags now, the last five yards of the pool, and he had already flipped, pushing off toward her. She had wandered from the middle of the lane toward the lane line, and his first stroke upon surfacing collided with hers. Their hands smacked each other's, the delicate bones, the tendons, the flesh aching deeply.

He began to tread water in place to keep his head above the surface. "I'm so sorry!," he said. "I wasn't paying attention."

She held onto the lane line with her good hand, and waved the smarting hand gently in the water, letting the coolness ease the ache. She shrugged. She saw his mouth moving and assumed he was apologizing. She made an apology of her own, her fingers fluttering, water droplets spraying over onto his hair.

"Oh, I'm sorry, really. Doubly so because you can't even understand me," he said. He smacked the water with his good arm, letting his frustration flow. He sank down eight feet and crouched on the bottom, then rose hugging his knees slowly, slowly. She hung onto the lane line with her good hand and dove down, meeting him halfway in the depths. He looked at her, frustrated at himself for blowing any chance of getting to know her, and he thought this. She heard him, and laughed lightly. "Oh he is nice," he heard her say. Her voice was pretty, light, innocent with disuse. Then she said, "Doesn't he believe in happy accidents?" They both shot to the surface, bewildered, confused, her hands fluttering, his mouth working, both in conversations neither would ever understand. They sank down again, to disappear from each other only to find that was where they understood each other best.

60:59:59

Lance R. was not much of a swimmer, but he didn't need to be. He simply swam a doggie-paddle, his best approximation of a competitive freestyle stroke, and tried to keep his mouth and ears underwater as much as possible. He willed himself to think only of the one thing that had been on his mind the past ten years: his high school sweetheart. They had broken up before graduation over some dumb high school argument he couldn't even remember (his Trans-Am? Her scholarship to fashion school?). Now she was back working at the town's hotspot, Thai Me Down restaurant, and Lance R. couldn't get his mind off her if he tried. Daily one or the other co-worker told him about their Pad Thai and his ex-girlfriend, how she made the best iced coffee or wrote the funniest things on their receipts. If Lance had one regret in his young life, losing her was it.

After a few laps the matronly woman swimming next to him had given Lance all the advice and moral support he needed, via this wonderful underwater world. He exited the pool, giddy, almost electrified, and finished the installation. He quit his job that week, drove immediately to the restaurant, and visited his sweetheart every day until she said 'yes.' They eventually married and fulfilled Lance R.'s lifelong dream of moving to New Zealand to raise sheep.

00:00:00

As the years went by people would often ask Lance and his wife how they got back together, how they moved to the underside of the world. His wife was still unclear about what prompted Lance to contact her, but she was too happy making noodles and goat milk soap to dwell on that unknown.

Lance, for his part, told everyone to study thunderstorms. They hold the key elements of attraction.

Pal Joey

Ronda Beaman

Looking at the CAT scan screen I think, "The Kardashians and *Real Housewives* got nothing. This is what they mean when they say Reality TV." I am blinking fast and furious faucets of tears hoping I can lift off and out of this cramped, over-heated office fueled solely by eyelash power. The young oncologist is calm. The scene, like his job, is a re-run, scripted with words like "cancer," "Stage 4," "8 months to a year," "so sorry", "do what we can."

The star of this show is my mother, gazing dispassionately at the display of her ravaged insides, deserving of an Emmy for her portrayal of the heroic patient who will triumph.

"I will treat you as if you were my own Mother," the doctor says as he puts his arm around her.

"I would rather have you treat me like I was your girlfriend… I think I'll get better care that way," she says as she turns her face upward, leans into his hug, bats her own eyelashes, and smiles.

Mother had played the role of beautiful wife for over 50 years. As a recent widow, now adrift, she committed that day to her metastases as she had her marriage — devoted, singular, brave, and with consistent humor.

"I cry alone," she whispered to me as I drove on the interminable ride back to her recently downsized modular home stuffed with her oversized furniture and personality.

I never heard her bemoan her fatal fate nor caught a glimpse of self-pity. She wore full force makeup and colorful clothes every day she had remaining. She planted perennials, and boasted to me, "This death sentence means bye-bye budget. I can buy two lipsticks at once if I want."

One morning I awoke to a frantic call, "I am dying, come get me, take me to the emergency room." I rushed over to find her waiting in her driveway wearing her full-length mink coat over silk pajamas and looking as pale as the paper on her lit cigarette.

"It's a Lucky Strike," she moaned as I helped her into the car. "A Lucky Strike! If that doesn't make me an oxymoron... maybe just a moron."

Her radiologist had failed to explain that the weekly treatments would constipate her. As stoic as she was glib, and armed with a daily morphine patch, she simply thought not going to the bathroom the past two weeks was a time-saving bonus.

The emergency room physician sent her immediately into surgery for fecal impaction.

"You are not the first to tell me I am full of shit," she told the surgeon before they put her under to remove eight pounds of waste.

Mother was an exemplar of the Kurt Vonnegut school of emotional riposte. "Laughter and tears," he said, "are both responses to frustration and exhaustion. I myself prefer to laugh, since there is less cleaning up to do afterward."

Sitting with her in the hospital room hours later she told me she had asked to see what was removed from her bowels.

"What?" I replied, aghast by the request, "Why in the world would you want to see... why for gawds sake would you want to look at, I mean... geezus, Mother!"

"It had a little face," she continued, "It even had little hairs."

Now past disgust, I was wincing.

"I named it Joey."

At that, my head snapped toward her. Our eyes locked and in an instant all the absurdities of life, death, cancer, mothers and daughters, indignities, triumphs, legacies, and loss reached a crescendo as we broke into raucous, cleansing, and healing laughter.

From that day on we named anyone rude to us a "Joey." We joked constantly that the whole damn cancer and everything that came with it was a ginormous pile of "Joey."

A day could be a "Joey."

Within six months, my Mother was dead. The cancer had spread throughout her body, into her spine and brain, bypassing only her funny bone.

None of us can know what will get us in the end. It will be Joey of some kind. I can only hope when my time comes I can honor what Mother taught me; be flush with humor, give pain a waggish name, and leave the legacy of a good laugh.

For Caleb Kosinski, Wherever He May Roam

Barbra Meri Frey

You are good. You are bad. You have a filthy, dirty mouth. You shame me beyond belief. You are fat. You are thin. Too thin. Why don't you eat? I'm eating. I'm having a ham and cheese—don't tell your mother. You've been nothing but a disappointment. A treasure. Who do you think you are, young lady? I don't recognize you anymore. You're not getting any younger, you know. And I'm not getting older. Who are you? You are me. And I love you very much.

I got the phone call at seven o-clock this morning. My father, Caleb—an insane man, a man for all seasons, a lover to his wife, a pain in the ass to his children—suffered a major coronary in the middle of the night. Mother called 911 and now Caleb is all doped up, lying in a bed at Mount Sinai. Prepare yourself, they tell me. They don't know whether he'll make it, they tell me. They just don't know.

My sister made the initial call, waking Bill, my soon to be ex-husband. I, too, was doped up—too dopey to hear the telephone ring. Painkillers. Lots of rest. I finished my last bout of chemo three weeks ago. They say I'm in remission. Still, I feel like shit. And when it comes down to it, my doctors said, they just don't know. They don't. We can make no guarantees, they said. It was ovarian. Very treatable nowadays. But then I think of Gilda Radner and I freak. Caleb's latest pep talk was just a week ago. You are a survivor, he said. A fighter. You are an amazing woman. I am so very proud of you.

The thought of my leaving the planet before he did completely flabbergasted him. Devastated him. When I was really ill back in September, my mother and Bill down in the hospital cafeteria, Caleb would sit by my side and hold my hand. He'd cry and smile at the same time, and think it was funny to raise the bed, lower the bed. I'm giving you a ride, he said. Where do you want to go?

Caleb and I have always gotten mixed reviews. We're more of a bad nightclub act than father and daughter. Pulling bunnies out of a hat and singing lousy

showtunes. He taught me everything I know—such a ham, my mother called
him Porky and me Petunia—until one day I began to teach him. I'm not sure of
the date but I can remember the pain. Chasing me around the house when I told
him to fuck off—age thirteen. The belt he'd threaten me with, and sometimes
use on the rare occasion he caught me. I'd take to the streets, running out in
my pajamas and he'd be there following behind—he was a runner, I was nine.
Running and screaming, screaming and running. We were famous, Caleb and
I. Very popular with the neighbors. Friends up the road would tease and say
how they could hear my voice while sitting on the toilet or taking a bath. They
thought it was hysterical. Caleb and I were a couple of Keystone Cops sent
for their amusement. Though it wasn't always amusing. Once he slammed me
against my bedroom door and gave me TMJ, the jaw disorder. He denies it to
this very day, but he knows. Deep down he does know. Then there was the time I
came home late from my shift at Burger King in the midst of a crazy snowstorm.
My boyfriend at the time, chief of the burger board and specialty sandwiches,
had a red Camaro and we were making out on the corner of my street. All of
a sudden there was Caleb in his bathrobe and galoshes, running toward us in
seven inches of snow, so pissed he was spitting.

Hurry! I told my boyfriend, but we were stuck on a snow bank and it was
too late. Charging Caleb pulled me out of the car by my hair—but not before
he shook hands with the Burger King and wished him well. As he dragged me
home I could see my mother and sister staring out the living room window—my
little sister crying. Caleb slapped the side of my head. Look at your sister. Your
mother. They thought you were dead. Unimaginable, I thought. Unthinkable. I
was fifteen.

If you get hold of Caleb's baby picture and set it next to mine, you won't be
able to tell us apart. No one can. We're identical.

It was never hatred with Caleb, just an all-consuming, overbearing love
that was so large, so massive, he didn't know what to do. Like a big dumb dog
slopping it up. Complete with hugs and kisses and persistence. He'd drive my
friends and I to the mall, wait three hours in the parking lot, and then drive
us home. Then there was the time I caught him standing in the corner of my
favorite teen nightclub, hiding near a bartender who was serving up virgin piña
coladas and apple juice. Dancing with my girlfriends, feeling real fine, I do one of
my famous spins and there he is: waving and smiling; he does a little dance.

He calls me several times a day—from his office, or from home, but down in the basement so my mother won't hear.

How you feeling, he'll ask. How you feeling now? Better than this morning? The day before?

He'll do the same to my sister but after the third call, she'll hit Do Not Disturb. His all-time high—16 calls within one 24-hour period. And that was just last week.

I take the Metro-North to the hospital. I made sure Bill didn't come. Caleb isn't particularly fond of Bill. In fact, he hates him. Always did. He thinks he's weak. A wuss. Another of my huge mistakes.

With this in mind, I travel alone, my bald head wrapped in a glittery scarf. I arrive in less than an hour and find myself in ICU, waiting my turn. The scene is too familiar; a combination of porridge and ammonia. Warm cans of Ensure. Again, I'm told that it's bleak, this time by one of the nurses. I send my mother down for coffee. My sister takes her. Intensive Care at Mount Sinai allows only one person at a time to keep vigil. I sit on the edge of his bed and hold his hand. Hey Caleb, I say, trying to wake him up. I think about giving him the old bed ride, but a nasty, hawk-eyed nurse shoots me the evil eye as if to say don't you dare. I poke him in the arm instead.

Wake up, Daddy. Come on get up—it's me.

And then suddenly he does. His eyes open and they're smiling. He calls me Madame Soutzaka in his thin, reedy voice and grabs hold of my wrist. We sit quietly for the longest time, neither of us saying a word. We stare into each other's eyes and wonder where we went wrong—all this sickness and disease; all this death.

This is the proper order of things. This is the way to go. Father then child. I swear he's doing it on purpose. It feels planned.

I'm sorry, he says. He knows that I'm angry, even though I cry.

Forgive me.

I shake my head. I refuse. I'm too afraid of what will happen next. I love you, Daddy. I say that instead.

No, forgive me, he says. The stubborn old fool. Forgive me, forgive me. He repeats it like a mantra until I can no longer bear it.

You're forgiven! I shout. I shout at my dying father, and he takes off, wearing a grateful little smile. Another battle won. Within moments, he is gone.

Hunger

Karen Guzman

He'd had to get out of Danbury. It was haunted. Since his mother died—his poor mother, bedridden and half bald—the streets of the little city were closing in on him. Every morning, guiding the delivery truck through the leafy old neighborhoods behind Main Street, Arthur had felt the weight of his failure. Each house he passed, all the tidy white Colonials and brick Georgians, accused him with their manicured yards and prim window shutters.

Well, he'd stayed too long. That was the problem. Just another fat man in a dead-end job, falling asleep in front of the television every night, filling the passenger seat of his car with McDonald's take-out bags.

Finding the job on Cape Cod had been easy. The Danbury paper where Arthur, at thirty-six, had spent his entire working life, had a sister paper on the Cape. This paper posted an opening for a driver, and he'd immediately e-mailed a letter to the circulation head and practically begged for the job. Then when they gave it to him, he discovered it was even better than he thought. He refilled honor boxes in the shopping strips that dot the lower Cape—Orleans and Falmouth and Buzzards Bay. No more driving up to houses, no more spotless yards and perfect lives glaring at him. With any luck, he spoke to one, maybe two, people each day: the guys who load the papers into the trucks.

Dear Lily,
You would no doubt be horrified to see my life now, so I take some measure of solace in knowing you never will. I'm sure you're married or at least engaged by now. Girls like you don't stay single. But people like me are evergreens. We're rooted. We stay and stay and stay until one day "poof" we're gone, and even then nobody really notices. So, despite your horror, I would like to remind you that a low profile is better than no profile at all.

He was a good writer. It was his secret vanity. He'd planned on becoming a journalist, only he'd ended up delivering newspapers instead of writing them.

He wrote Lily these letters now, sitting at his kitchen table—his mother's old card table with the folding metal legs.

He never mailed the letters. He stuck them in one of the kitchen's empty drawers.

Cape Cod in winter was magical, glassy and pristine, with frost glittering on the village greens, smoke curling into the air from brick chimneys and miles of hard-packed, windswept beaches, empty of tourists and clatter. The cold air and water swept in and purified, lying bare the stark outline of the coast.

This beauty stirred Arthur. He felt it like an ache, an unbearable longing, almost the way he felt about food. That was something Lily never understood. He ate because he needed to. Food transported him, if only for a few minutes. The price for this was being fat. Well, it was a rigged system. It wasn't his fault. It wasn't anybody's fault.

He had mashed potatoes for dinner. Sometimes a whole box of instant Hungry Jack with a stick of butter and a bulb of garlic. Food never made him sick. He could tolerate the oddest combinations. Scrambled eggs and tuna fish. Pizza and blueberry pie. Green olives sprayed with whipped cream out of a can. Until tonight.

The mashed potatoes were burning a hole through his chest. He belched and felt the renegade potatoes brimming at the back of his throat. He swallowed and belched again. God, so loud. He pushed himself back from the table. A walk in the cold night air was what he needed. He ventured out at night sometimes, walking to the village center or to the harbor.

He bundled up in his blue down parka and ski cap, opened the apartment door and clomped down the wooden steps. The entrance hall and front porch were empty, the driveway still. The faint thump of Dick's machine drifted through the building. Dick, who must have been in his early sixties, had some kind of medical condition. A rickety-looking fellow with an ashy gray complexion, he had a huffy way of breathing. Every night he ran some sort of whirring, thumping machine in his apartment.

Outside the night was sharply cold. Every detail—the faded wooden rails around a neighbor's yard, the pointed needles of the pines clustered near the mailbox—stood out in sharp relief.

Arthur's breath came in puffs as he trudged along the sandy shoulder and stepped onto the sidewalk where the road grew broader nearing the village center. Porch lights glowed at the homes he passed. He could see the flickering light of a television screen through one window. In another, a man and two children sat around a table, laughing.

The flagpole on the village green was just ahead. It was late January. Coming to the Cape, Arthur had hoped to dissolve into the monotony of his days and nights, to fade out. Only he hadn't. He'd never been able to. In elementary school when the teasing became unbearable—Fat Ass Arty, they called him—he would go to the boys' bathroom, lock himself into a stall, close his eyes and hold as still as he could.

By high school, he had mastered the ability to move through the halls, blocking out everything. Sometimes he went an entire day without speaking to anyone.

Then his father, who was also fat, died. Arthur came home from school to find his sister nearly catatonic on the living room couch and his mother frantically scrubbing the kitchen floor. "People will be here after the funeral," she said. "They'll all come here. What are they going to think?"

Arthur had retreated to his bedroom and closed the door. After midnight he snuck down to the kitchen and, standing barefoot in the dark, ate half an apple pie.

Somehow they all went on. Arthur graduated high school, tried community college, and made a few stabs at the student newspaper. He was too paralyzed with embarrassment to approach the young women who caught his eye, too tired and disgusted to figure it out. Then Lily came along and look how that had ended.

He reached the harbor and sat on a wooden bench facing the sea. It was breezy, colder. He pulled his ski cap down over his ears. A few fishing boats, nets and buckets on their decks, bobbed and creaked among the docks. The bright windows of the Dockside Pub shone. This was where the locals went to eat chowder, throw darts, and cheer the Celtics and Patriots. On game nights, the windows vibrated with shouts.

He composed a letter in his mind.

Dear Lily,

Remember your apartment on the riverbank in Danbury? The silver wind chimes you kept in every window? On nice days you'd open the windows, and the apartment would fill with that mysterious tinkling. You called it the breath of God. I called it a noisy racket. I wonder how you stood me as long as you did.

"Art?"

Arthur jumped and swung his head around.

"We thought it was you, Dude." It was one of the guys from the apartment beneath his. A couple of young fishermen in their twenties lived together downstairs. They rose before dawn every morning, fired up their truck and rattled off to the docks.

"We just docked," said Henry, the tall slender one. "Damn, what a rough day. The surf's a nightmare out there. It was like getting fucked on a roller coaster."

"That's what your mother said last night."

This was Andy, the short one who was always yelling in the front yard. He had a black buzz-cut that made him look military. Arthur preferred Henry who had a mop of brown curls and tendency to flush red in the face.

"Have a beer with us, Arty," Henry said. "We're going to the Dockside."

"Well, I was just sitting here, and…"

"Beer, big guy. Come on," Andy coaxed. "A nice foamy brewski."

"I was experiencing some, um, indigestion before."

"Beer's healthy," Andy said.

"Don't twist the man's arm," Henry said. "We can grab a beer any night."

"Yes," Arthur said. "Absolutely. Just knock on my door."

Arthur watched as they headed down the sidewalk and disappeared into the pub. A crystal flurry began falling from the sky.

He fried pork chops the next night. They were sizzling in the black skillet atop the white stove when he felt the first pain. It was a dull contraction, almost like a tiny hand deep inside his chest had grabbed hold of something. A sour taste rose like lava in his throat. A burning tingling ran down his left arm. He paused, put one hand on his chest and inhaled. A pork chop hissed and popped, and a drop of grease shot onto his white t-shirt.

He exhaled slowly. It was the indigestion acting up again, no doubt. Though the arm tingling was new, and weird. It subsided. He went back to the chops, poking one with a fork and flipping it over. A shower of grease bullets burned his arm, and he pulled it away. Then his arm exploded in a missile of pain.

Arthur backed away from the stove and fell to his knees. He swayed, then dropped flat on his back, eyes squeezed shut. The pain was remarkable, cleaving his chest in half. He couldn't get enough air. He felt like he was breathing through a straw. Another stab ripped his chest. He pounded the floor with his fist—the cold, cheap linoleum floor. His mother had linoleum on the kitchen floor, too, until the end. There had once been talk of redoing the house. His mother fell in love with a rust-colored ceramic floor tile in the local hardware store. He wanted to buy it, to redo the kitchen as a Christmas gift. But she suddenly lost interest. He left college at the end of the term and found the newspaper delivery job. No one passed judgment. If you never really expect anything, you can't be disappointed.

This is how he would be found: lying dead on the kitchen floor in boxer shorts and a t-shirt splattered with pork chop grease. He opened his eyes and stared at the creamy ceiling. His heart was jabbing and skittering in his chest. What had Lily ever seen in him? He was starting to forget her, the lilt of her voice, her soft step beside him. She was disappearing. Tears burned his eyes. Another blow hit his chest. He bellowed like a great, beached leviathan, like one of those poor pilot whales that strand themselves on the Cape's hard-packed beaches.

Someone was pounding on the door. "Art, it's Dick from upstairs. I heard some awful shouting. Are you there?"

"I'm here," Arthur croaked. "Please help. I'm alone."

There was a scuffling. Someone galloped up the stairs, the fishermen. Something hit the door with tremendous force. Arthur was sweating. Bitterness filled his mouth. He saw the silver rings flashing on Lily's fingers, saw his mother drifting through the halls of the old house, her bedroom slippers slapping the floorboards. Then the fishermen were above him, their flushed, anxious faces. Dick was talking into his phone. The fishermen were pulling him into the living room, throwing a blanket around him, patting his back, saying everything would be alright.

He didn't die. Why would he, when living held infinitely more possibilities for struggle? And maybe none was more persistent than this physical therapist, Laura. She set a course for his "recovery goals," or rather they set it together, with her needling "How do you see your life? Where would you like to take your body?" He wanted to take it home. He longed for his couch, for the remote control. It was bad enough that he couldn't eat the foods he enjoyed, bad enough that he choked down pills every morning, but the physical therapy was torture. He'd already been through cardiac rehab. Now he met Laura three days a week at Harborside Physical Therapy. She was a nutritionist, too.

"Fifteen minutes on the treadmill, Art?" she said.

He lumbered over to the machine, feeling conspicuous in his stiff, new gray sweat suit and blinding white sneakers. The gym section was a large open room with a few treadmills, stationery bicycles, and weight lifting contraptions.

Arthur pounded away on the treadmill while Laura watched the blinking heart rate monitor on the machine's screen. She was a quiet, calm woman. She had shoulder-length brunette hair and a fringe of bangs over her smooth forehead.

She seemed never to doubt that he would lose the 100-plus pounds the doctor recommended. She wore a brilliant platinum band with an icy diamond on her left ring finger. Arthur heard the receptionists talking about it. Laura was a widow. Her young husband was killed a few years back when the towers fell in New York. Now she was engaged to one of the doctors at the local hospital.

"That's fifteen," she said. "Good job." She pressed the button that slowed the treadmill. Her diamond flashed.

"Nice ring," he said. He came to a stand still, horrified at whatever possessed him to say that.

"Thank you. I, we, just got engaged last month."

"That's, uh, wonderful."

"I never thought I'd be doing this again," she said.

"I was engaged once, but we had to call it off," he said.

Lily and he had never been engaged.

"I'm sorry," Laura said. "Who called it off? You or her?"

"Me."

Another lie. He hadn't called anything off; he'd simply given up.

Sunlight streamed through the window into Laura's face. Gold flecks dotted the brown irises of her eyes.

"I did what I thought I had to do," he said. His voice sounded detached, as if it were coming from someone else's body. "It was all I knew."

Laura put a hand his shoulder. He felt the weight of it, firm and present. He stared down at the black rubber of the treadmill.

Dear Lily,

I feel like a jigsaw puzzle full of chipped pieces. Nothing fits together anymore. All my life I've only wanted to be safe. Was that a mistake? You would say yes. I can hear you. And here's something else, something you really should know: I heard you back then, too.

By spring, he'd lost forty pounds, not all he needed to lose, but enough to make a difference. He noticed it walking and climbing stairs, a new ease, lightness. The wretched treadmill and endless salads—salad with grilled shrimp, with grilled chicken, with every manner of bean and sprout—were paying off. He still longed for juicy red steaks and steaming bowls of pasta. But to his surprise, he was not hungry. He had learned to distinguish what real hunger was and how easily it could be satisfied. It seemed to him now he had never truly been hungry. He had simply been eating.

"I went to the grocery store and bought all the fresh vegetables you suggested," he told Laura in her office.

She was in on all his secrets, the eating binges and how he liked to walk at night to avoid people, how when he topped the scales at nearly 300 pounds he had used a safety pin to hold his pants closed.

She stood. "Hey, I have something for you." She took a creamy envelope off her desk and handed it to him. "Wedding invitation," she said. "Come. Bring a good gift." She laughed. "And bring a date."

His eyes darted to her face, but he could see that she wasn't kidding. She saw him this way, as someone who could get a date, as someone with options. Someone else had tried to pull back the top of his head and yell this inside, too. Lily. Yes, Lily.

"Uh, thank you," he said. "I'll see if ... I'll RSVP you." He slipped the envelope in his pocket.

Afterward he drove to the beach. In late April the first warm breaths of spring were stirring over the Cape. Songbirds whistled and peeped in the branches, gulls swooped low, crying over the sand. A fecund, salty scent hung in the air, and the sea stirred with secret, new life. Arthur stood at the surf's edge. The sky soared away above him, blue and perfect, rolling out to meet the horizon.

He squinted and could make out a few boats far off shore, boxy vessels, fishing boats probably. He wondered if Henry and Andy were out there, casting their nets. They had rushed to his apartment that terrible night and broken down the door. They had stayed with him, waiting for the ambulance. One of them dug a pair of pants out of the laundry basket so he could cover his boxer shorts.

Arthur's arms shot into the air. He waved them overhead, as if he were trying to hail the boats.

"Hey," he boomed. Foolish, no one could hear. "Hey, Guys," he called against the wind.

The boats inched along the horizon line. Arthur lowered his arms. Energy pulsed through him. The forty fewer pounds must have improved his blood flow. He would ask Laura. She would know.

He marched up the beach. He felt like he could walk all day. He could lap the perimeter of the Cape, going beach-to-beach, along the Atlantic and then in around the bays. His heart beat solidly. He imagined his arteries, the sticky gunk of his life lining them and the medicine beating it back now.

Dear Lily, little by little I can almost feel it disappearing.

He fingered Laura's invitation in his pocket and saw himself there—this ex-fat guy raising a glass of champagne. He gazed out over the waves, across the bold shifting face of the sea, to the rest of the world.

The Nose Always Points North

Jenna R. London

Moonbeam danced along snow, casting shadows of white pine and black birch. Clouds drifted across sky. Hayduke and I suited up. I clipped the orange vest—with SEARCH AND RESCUE stitched in black in two spots—around his furry black and white body. Three lights the size of fifty-cent pieces dangled in the center and on both sides. A fourth light hung from the red collar around Hayduke's neck. I secured my pack and tightened the shoulder strap.

Eight of us—a ragtag group of outdoor junkies who preferred the company of dogs to most people—were members of the Lower Adirondack Search and Rescue Team's canine sector. Karen, the de facto team expert and leader (I secretly called her Alpha Human) would decide tonight if Hayduke and I should advance to the next stage in certification.

I couldn't screw us up. I couldn't miss a hint from Hayduke indicating he found scent, no matter how subtle he was, no matter how hard I struggled to see my black dog at night, and no matter how deep the snow drifts ran. I couldn't lose track of where I'd been, or what wind had been doing. I couldn't forget to give Hayduke a water break, even if he didn't want one. I couldn't give Karen the opportunity to hold us back any longer. As a pair and as individuals, Hayduke and I had worked too hard to fail.

I was a few months past 30 years old. As a wetland biologist for the power company, I'd arranged a work transfer from a seaside town—Plymouth, Massachusetts—to one near the mountains in Saratoga Springs, New York. My boyfriend, Phil, a fellow biologist, planned on moving with me. But once it was imminent, he dumped me instead.

Less than a month after I moved—alone—I adopted Hayduke. A couple months after that, I joined Search and Rescue, my primary motivation being to find a group in which I truly belonged. But I stood out because I was the youngest by ten years. Hayduke was the only mutt. We were the only pair not from Upstate New York. Hayduke was the only dog who hadn't had training or health issues delay his progress. I was the only one comfortable navigating off trail with either a map and compass or a GPS.

Hayduke and I were misfits among misfits. As the only field team happy to participate in extended projects that kept us in the woods a long way from home, Phil and I had been the misfits among misfits among our co-workers, too. This identity haunted me my entire life. Then Hayduke came along and taught me it was a gift.

The team had arrived a few hours before dark to train the other dogs. Once the animals had water and were settled into their respective vehicles, Sally, the assistant canine officer, volunteered to wait with them. The rest of us would walk a seventy-acre area while Hayduke and I looked for Nelson, my "subject" (the name given to the person who hid), who'd hiked about an hour ago into a location unknown to me. Karen had given me a paper map with my search grid sketched in black. This area had also been programmed into her GPS.

Parting clouds revealed moon. I'd long ago programmed myself to note the Northern Cross and Big and Little Dippers. I didn't ask if anyone else noticed these winter constellations. The search area was bounded to the north, south, and west by hiking trails and by a stream to the east. In search and rescue, these boundaries were called bump lines. Orienting north was the most common practice. But mostly I'd count on Hayduke's nose to find our subject.

Once everyone was ready, we headed across the parking lot.

"We'll be back!" Karen called to Sally.

"Watch out for weirdos in the woods!" Sally responded.

"Look at us," I said to Karen. "Saturday night, we're running around in freezing cold with lights and compasses and GPS's and dog toys hanging from our jackets. I think we *are* the weirdos in the woods."

"You have a point," she said. For once, she laughed. Though I always longed for acceptance in a group, I'd simply felt most comfortable around animals and in the woods.

We walked to the trail's edge. I turned my attention to Hayduke. He trotted in half-moons. His vest and my pack were triggers for him, not to mention the fact that he'd spent hours in the back of our small SUV watching his dog buddies head to work. But he'd wait until I gave him the command, and even then Hayduke sometimes took a few minutes to focus. Who didn't get distracted at night in woods, when fresh snow blanketed earth and stars provided all the light one needed? Was more than coincidence involved when Hayduke's forever home was with a person in love with nature?

Now those winter nights stay rooted in my soul as part of who I was rather than who I currently am. And I wish Hayduke could use words to tell me what he thinks of the time he was a Search and Rescue dog—the best on the team. How could those hours in the woods have not instilled the same sense of confidence and empowerment they'd instilled in me?

In a real search scenario, a canine team was composed of the handler, dog and one flanker—someone to work the radio, to offer moral support, and to document wind direction. Occasionally, someone else would come along to observe or to practice navigation skills. The handler—in this case, me—was supposed to walk a few paces ahead.

Search and rescue dogs are trained in either air scent or tracking. Give a tracking (also called trailing) dog a glove or a hat from the subject, and, working on a leash, the pooch will follow the general path the subject has taken. The leash is attached to the center of the dog's search harness and not from the collar around his neck so that he won't hurt himself when he pulls at the leash. But if stormy weather ruins the track, or if many hours have passed, most trailing dogs can't work. Therefore, they are most often used in urban settings for Alzheimer's patients and children.

Hayduke and I were too wild to traipse through woods on a leash, so we trained for air scent. These search dogs are not scent specific and are most often used in rugged terrain to cover long distances. Because of this, their handlers are required to take additional tests to prove efficiency with a map, compass, and GPS. But no matter the specialty, well-trained dogs suited for search and rescue are like a bunch of Albert Einsteins with four legs and a tail—geniuses able to process information the average person couldn't fathom. And while I watched these animals communicate without words, my own pain dissipated into the woods Hayduke and I wandered though.

I needed a forward-moving dog and could never work well with the kind who had to be convinced not to quit. Hayduke needed a forward-moving person, too. He got aggravated if I took excessive breaks to check the wind or my map. He'd circle me. He'd woof quietly or thwack a stick back and forth against the ground, which looked completely different from when he wanted me to throw a stick for him when he was playing. I remained intrigued by how personality traits Hayduke and I shared presented themselves in him. When I was impatient, I'd tap my foot or fidget, but I supposed whacking a stick would work, too.

That night, six people would be coming with Hayduke and me. I'd expected Karen—the evaluator—and maybe one other person, two at the absolute most. But a whole crew? Never. I wasn't much of a conspiracy theorist, but her actions did make me wonder if she was trying to show her dominance or remind me who was in charge. *She's setting us up to fail*, I thought. Now, as I write this, I am even more sure Alpha Human was trying to take me down a notch for reasons that probably didn't even have much to do with me. But regardless of her motivation, Karen and I both knew that keeping a large group close together at night in snow over rugged terrain was nearly impossible. Since Hayduke wasn't scent-specific, he could easily pick up a group member if the individual fell far enough behind me. I wasn't supposed to have to worry about anyone or anything else except wind and my dog.

I stopped when we reached the trail, knelt on the ground to orient my map north and figure out which compass bearing I needed to follow to get to the stream on the other end of our search area. I flicked my lighter to check the wind. A slight breeze wafted across my face, coming east. Perfect. Karen asked me what my search plan would be.

"Well, we're here." I pointed to the western bump line. "And wind's coming from here," I pointed again. "So I'm going to get us to the middle of that bump line and see if my little hoodlum's gotten any scent and I'll go from there."

"Okay. Good job," she said. "I like that approach. And your breeze is real nice. It's 8:14. If you can find him in an hour you'll be in really good shape."

I nodded. *We can do this.*

"Hayduke, come." I stood tall and squared my shoulders. He bounded over to me—tongue hanging out, mouth forming a smile, eyes wide open and alert, tail swishing back and forth.

"Sit." I pointed to my side. I scratched his head twice from his eyes to his ears. "Okay, Hayduke."

I drew my right pointer finger from his nose to woods in front of us.

"Go find him!"

We were off, headed north.

What I saw on a winter night when my dog was in front of me was more like art than real life. My black dog reflected off white snow. His feet and stocky body forged through it. His body language—standing at attention, nose in the air, and tail up—gave me messages. Like a compass arrow adhering to its draw to magnetic north, Hayduke and I connected with one another. He'd shift direction when he had scent. I'd keep us within our search grid, reining him in by adjusting my pace.

What I saw on a winter night when I considered my dog's behavior an art form was easier to interpret than when I thought of him as an animal unable to speak words and therefore unable to communicate.

What I saw on a winter night was that snow was gorgeous and amazing—how could no flake ever be the same?

A few dead beech leaves, still attached to their branch, swayed gently in the breeze—the ideal wind speed for searching. Light from moon as it reflected off snow made my headlamp unnecessary. I double-checked my compass bearing, but my heart always pointed north when we worked. I could only go so far into the deepest forest before I would come out the other side. An overwhelming feeling of inclusion and contentedness consumed me when I was alone with my dog in woods at night.

Now the snag of dead trees—our first landmark, about half a mile north of where we'd started—was within arm's reach. Hayduke worked in large half-moons into wind, nose up, filtering information sent to him by breeze. I lined up my compass again, ready to pick another landmark. But Hayduke's lights stopped moving. I saw his outline—sitting with perfect posture, ears perked forward and in line with his haunches, shoulders squared, back straight, staring ahead. Some dogs would subtly sniff or shake their head when they found scent. But part of why Hayduke was a great search and rescue dog was because he gave distinct indications. If he ever doubted himself, I didn't know it.

Hayduke sat with his nose pointed north, and I knew he'd caught a whiff of scent from that direction. It hadn't been strong enough to pinpoint. But my dog at least knew what the subject smelled like. I'd love to have been included in his thought process in those moments his nose took over.

This was a winter night when even bears and foxes slept. Only weirdos would be out. Since our group filled that role, I was confident Hayduke had smelled his subject and nobody else. He looked over his shoulder at me. Through dark and snow and branches and pine needles, we made eye contact. The moment was too pure for me to second guess either one of us. Hayduke trotted west. I abandoned my plan of following my compass bearing. I needed to follow my dog. Karen, still a couple of feet behind me, piped in.

"Now, what do you think …wah, wah, wah?" I pretended her words sounded like adults on the *Peanuts* cartoon. I wasn't trying to be rude. She was deciding whether or not to recommend us for the next level. If she were setting me up for success she'd have stood back and let me work my dog. So why was Karen distracting me at this juncture? Could she really want me to fail?

I banished this question, forced her voice to blend with breeze, picked up my pace, and lengthened my stride. Hayduke and I needed to succeed tonight. I couldn't let my mind get cluttered with other thoughts. I was paying attention to twists and turns we'd taken, the ridgeline and small wetland behind us. How could it all look peaceful and haunting at the same time?

I didn't know where we were in relation to the bump line—the boundary of my search grid. I'd have to look at the map. But I wasn't ready to stop walking.

I needed to anticipate what my dog needed. Hayduke would figure out the hard part—finding human scent amid many acres and smells of animals, birds, leaves, bark, bugs, worms, and moss on stones. But when breeze stopped or swirled in multiple directions, it was my job to help us by walking, zigging and zagging our way through Adirondack woodlands and along streams and around rock ledges until wind picked up again and Hayduke found our subject.

Hayduke bailed us out of a lot of situations, more than other dogs did. I'd miss a head pop—a quick pause in his action and his head would turn in the direction of scent—and move us out of an area but Hayduke would drag us back with his nose, finding the well-hidden subject hiding under a thick bramble of picker bushes.

When wind changed direction, Hayduke often adjusted his approach without my guidance. Sometimes I'd stand in one spot for a while, staying out of the way and giving him the chance to work out whatever information bombarded his olfactory senses. Trusting others wasn't my forte—especially given the recent breakup—so having this sort of relationship with my dog was a good but foreign feeling. As important as it was for Hayduke and I to rely on one another, I can only realize now that in order to develop trust, both of us had to know how to understand and follow our individual instincts, too.

Trusting my dog made me nervous for reasons that seem backwards to me now. What would happen when Hayduke wouldn't be able to bail us out? Surely that day would come. Did I have what it took to turn the situation around and make our search successful? By learning to trust my dog, I was also able to hide my lack of self-confidence.

I didn't expect to feel as united with Hayduke and as secure in my own capabilities as I did that January night. It was as if there had been a blip in the cosmic cycle and for that time, Hayduke and I worked as one. Hayduke was an extension of my nose. I was an extension of his inner compass. The wind danced in front of us. He worked and I followed him, giving him berth when I thought he needed it. In this cosmic blip, Hayduke shared his thoughts with me.

The wind sunk. Let's go down low. When wind slowed, so did Hayduke. He looked over his shoulder. *I lost him. I'm still trying.* He ran up a short hill then jumped on a few stumps to get his nose high in the air (a sign of his canine instinct revealing itself—this was not something I taught him to do). I paused only when I flicked my lighter to assess wind speed. It had picked up—around eight miles per hour now—and also changed directions every couple minutes, an aspect that was particularly confusing for a dog. Hayduke came trotting back. He tapped his nose against my lower thigh. *I need a drink.*

Maybe the subject, Nelson, had stopped to tie his shoe, or had backtracked, causing scent to pool in one area. Maybe Hayduke had made a mistake. But if the latter was correct, he didn't seem frustrated. For a human, it was hard to search without considering where the subject would hide. But thoughts like, *she wouldn't walk all the way up that slope,* or *he'd never cross the stream* almost always led to long, unsuccessful searches and missed areas.

That night when Hayduke came back to me, I knew even though wind had changed direction he didn't want to backtrack. I had to trust my dog, never guessing, then, that this trust in one another would stay with us long after his search and rescue days had ended. He sat at my feet, panting. I tossed his portable water dish on the ground. I filled it with my water bottle before taking a swig for myself. Hayduke drank, then rested. This was no ordinary jaunt in woods. Searching was mentally and physically exhausting for Hayduke—his millions of olfactory nerves worked in overdrive. My body probably could have used some food, but I was so focused on finding our hider that I couldn't be bothered. Searching was enough nourishment for me, anyway.

"I think I see Duke's lights all the way up there. He's not moving, though." My flankers were catching up.

"Yeah—there they are. I told you Jenna doesn't let snow settle under her feet." Karen's squeaky snowshoe kept tune with their conversation. I bumped against a sugar maple sapling and snow from its branch flittered to the ground. Nature gave me another barrier between people who appeared to be positive influences but who were actually the opposite.

"Well, it is a test. She's supposed to follow her dog."

"And jeeze, that dog is fast." Their voices carried loud and clear through the night. When I joined Search and Rescue, I didn't expect to be out of place because I was sure-footed in woods or because I could always pinpoint my location on a map. I was sure my crippling doubt—invisible to everyone but me—also set me apart. But now I understand that people drawn to these types of activities are often familiar with feelings of crippling self-doubt: the feelings simply reveal themselves in different ways.

Normally, by now I'd have convinced myself we'd walked past the subject, and I'd be more concerned about wind continuously shifting directions. Normally, I'd be sure I missed something—a signal from Hayduke, a reflection off the subject, a dip in terrain that could hide scent, or walking past the subject himself— because of the added challenge of darkness. Normally, I wouldn't have put such a distance between the rest of the group and me. Normally, I would have wondered if the group was okay.

But this wasn't a normal night.

I pulled the map out of my back pocket and oriented myself. I decided we would walk east for a couple hundred feet and stay below the ridgeline, since wind sunk at night. I picked up the water dish and stashed it. Hayduke sat, glanced at the mob of headlamps coming closer then back at me. He didn't want company, either.

"Okay, Dukey. Don't worry." I scratched behind his ear. "We'll get him." My confidence never soared more than in those serene moments with Heyduke in the woods.

"Ready? Go find him." I pointed again.

The lights and conversation of my herd of flankers faded into the night.

Hayduke found scent within twenty seconds. Wind swirled. I followed my dog.

He picked up his pace, head reached out straight, ears up. I felt wind shift as we reached ridgeline. I stayed low; Hayduke started up high. But when he was about halfway down the hillside, his lights blurred as he charged directly north through snow. He returned to view about thirty seconds later, bounding towards me with that hell-bent look on his face, eyes focused on the rope toy hanging from my belt loop.

"Whatcha got? Show me!" He snatched the toy off its Velcro strap and sprinted back where he'd come from—a few hundred feet away—across a trail, down an embankment. He jumped through snow, over roots and fallen trees. I followed after him, jogging as much as my snowshoes allowed.

"Yahooo! You found him! Good boy, Dukey!" Once I cheered, Nelson, the subject who'd bundled himself in a winter sleeping bag, sat, praised Hayduke and played tug with him—the ultimate reward. I pulled a cheese stick from my pack, unwrapped it and handed it to Nelson to feed to my pup. We emphasized the concept of subject loyalty, teaching the dog to stay with the subject and handler rather than charging through the woods on a victory lap. By the time Hayduke had finished his snack and was waiting for me to pour him some water, the rest of the group had arrived. They fussed over him, too.

"Now tell me where we are on the map," the Alpha said, anxious to grill me, once she'd caught up. Although we both knew she had a terrible sense of direction and equally terrible GPS skills, she falsely claimed to hold her own when a map and compass were involved. Her voice cut through my layers, grated on my nerves again. My utopia was shattered.

"We started over there. Went up that ridge… down that slope." My finger traced the path we'd walked. "So we must be right there." I pointed to a spot more than one-hundred feet outside the search area. "Wait. No. Yeah." I second-guessed myself because we weren't in the grid. My own sense of direction was something I'd developed over time and I prided myself on using land features like elevation, ridges, streams, and wetlands to orient myself to where I was on the paper to landscape I'd seen, my own inner compass able to orient itself when I felt freest.

"Yeah. That's where we are. Isn't it?" My brain was experiencing an optical illusion. There was no way we could be anyplace else. But why would we be out of the search grid? Now I can remind myself that even a compass went out of whack when it crossed hemispheres.

"Well, what do you think?" Karen always looked smug when I second-guessed myself.

"Okay. Yep. This is it. It has to be. This is my answer. This is where we are." I held the map out to her with my finger pointed to our location.

"No-ope." she said when she saw me pointing outside the search area. "Well. Let me see." Karen glanced at the spot and compared that to the blinking cursor— signifying our current location—on her GPS. "Oh. Hmmm. Yeah. Well, you're right. Your subject was hiding outside your search area." She whispered, "That's not where I told him to be." Then she spoke in her regular annoying voice, "But that's the kind of thing that could happen on a real search. He wasn't too far outside." Our momentary silence was thick with awkwardness until she filled it. Hayduke thwacked a stick against the ground.

"Not bad. You finished in twenty-eight minutes." Alpha Human shrugged, then busied herself rooting through her pack. "I'll let Rita know you're ready." She walked away, leaving me standing in the same spot, momentarily dumbfounded. She'd dismissed the fact that we'd found the subject in less than half the time allotted, even though Nelson was out of my search area and the wind had worked against us. What was her deal?

Once the massive group of flankers was ready to return to the parking lot, I called Hayduke and he bounded through snow to me, his tongue hanging out and the corners of his mouth upturned in delight. I kneeled on the ground to remove his vest, hugged him, and sighed. We'd been the only two beings on earth with trees, stars, shadows, moon, snow, rocks, and wind as our audience. But once the cheers had started Hayduke and I had been ripped out of our trance. It was jarring for me to return to reality, and I wondered if Hayduke felt the same way. He rested against my arms for a few seconds, breathing rhythmically. I buried my face in his long hair, frosty with cold as we helped each other back to real life with other people. I thought I was just trying to keep my brokenhearted-self busy when I adopted a dog and joined Search and Rescue. I never comprehended that that mass of fur would change the trajectory of how I view myself and my place in the world.

In the woods the night we passed our test, I headed along the unlit trail to the parking lot. My Dukey bounded in snow around me. To us, the rest of the group faded into the darkened forest again. A girl and her dog. A couple of weirdos in woods. Victorious misfits among misfits.

To the Farm

William Lychack

Funny the things that come back to you. I'm standing in Putnam Supermarket the other day, little old lady just minding my own business, just waiting in line at the deli counter, couple of guys getting sandwiches in front of me, and then all of a sudden past the lobsters I see this other tank all dark and green. Few steps closer, few more, and my stomach goes with the pull—*whole tank filled with eels*—black and squirming against the glass, that raw stink of river and weeds, and this urge rising from inside my throat.

Comes out half-laugh, half-groan—and the men at the counter turn and smile—I'm over by the tanks at this point, arms open wide to the men, asking what kind of *person*? I mean, who in their right mind would *eat* these things, anyway?

Guys all grin like I'm a little crazy maybe—which is fine by me, don't care what anyone thinks anymore, have come to embrace this cranky-old-woman-ness of mine—man behind the counter wrapping the sandwiches, saying he's had them before, the eels, they're not so bad.

To which I say, *Bahhh!*

And they laugh—and now I drift back—and I start to tell how, once upon a time, back when we lived on the Shetucket River, my husband used to run drop lines off the dock, bits of fresh chicken on the hooks every morning. Who knows, I say, but I think he was thinking turtles. All I know is I'm home from work one day, sunny summer afternoon down by the water, and somehow I get it in my head to see if anything's on the line. Bob's not home, naturally, so I'm there on the dock alone, expecting weeds or bad chicken on the hook, and then something starts fighting and fighting. Line goes all zigzagging and sharp, and I'm pulling it closer and leaning down for one last heave—when *foop!*—this big cold splash wraps itself wet and heavy *around my arm!*

Oh, I start *screaming*—and *keep* screaming—am slapping and hollering at the thing, its head tucking up under my arm, Bob rolling into the yard just about here, man running down to the river to me, me gasping to him about snakes, my knees trembling as Bob uncoils the thing from my arm, him laughing how that's no snake, Anna!

Ha, ha, ha, ha, ha—height of fricken hysterical to everyone—becomes the story of the eel in my bathroom, creature taking up residence for the night, floating almost three foot long, ring of grease on the sides of the tub, and the musk of it, Bob asking the eel if she might like some candles and a glass of wine.

Now you *know* I'm a madwoman by morning! Yelling for him to get that effen thing out of my house! Take it up to the farm! Swear I'll pour bleach on it! Swear I'll pour ammonia! Vow great harm upon the eel *and* him!

What a sight I must have been—both then and now—and these guys at the deli are all smiles as I tell this. It's one of those perfect moments in life, everything making brief and beautiful sense in the world, me saying, Sure gotta love an old bitty riled up over nothing, don't you?

Sure, sure, they say—and we're all laughing and happy—these guys with their sandwiches asking what happened next?

Well, I say, what d'you *think* happened next? I mean, what d'you think *always* happened next? I tell my husband to get that goddamned creature out of my house, and he yeah-yeahs himself off to work early—man never went to work early a day in his *life*—the eel looking like she's just gonna loll another day in my bathtub. All comfy, but I've got news for her and pull the plug and go about my business. Get dressed, start laundry, do dishes, whistle while I work, and when I check back on the progress of my eel's death? Can guess what happened next, can't you?

Guys look to one another, shrug they don't know, everyone glancing to the deli meats, the dairy section, entire supermarket leaning close to hear.

Well, I say—and I get all quiet and whispery—when I go back to look, I tell them, *the thing is gone!* Bathtub's empty and I'm standing there as if to calculate the drain, thinking *no fricken way,* no way an eel could fit down that hole. I'm staring as if to put it all together. Greasy ring around my tub, bar of soap in the dish, taste of river in the room, and then something *brushes my feet!*

Oh, I jump and scream all over again—thing lashing itself across the floor toward the toilet—and I'm pure hysteria and go for the paint thinner and Ajax and anything else under the sink that might be harmful. I'm pouring out shampoo and rubbing alcohol when Bob comes waltzing home—man forever swooping in for the highlights—says he only ran to the hardware store and flower shop and has, of all things, a bundle of flowers for me.

Laughs in a way that makes the flowers not count for shit—and I throw them back in his face—and Bob goes about scooping the eel into a garbage bag, singsonging that his wife's just crazy-crazy-crazy-crazy-crazy-crazy-crazy. Laughs his sorry ass all the way up to the farm, where he can clean and cook and choke to death on the bones of the thing for all I care.

Guys in the deli smile and wait for more—but that's all she wrote, I tell them—and soon it's down the cereal aisle they go, leaving me with the deli guy, man behind the counter asking what can he get for me. Half-pound of honey ham, I say, half-pound of salami, half-pound of provolone.

Still have eels on the brain when I get home—the eel, the farm, the house on the Shetucket River, all those years in Baltic washing ashore to me now—time I backed the car over the embankment, way Bob died on the couch, bowl of ice cream on his lap. A person could sit half the night like this, amazed by what returns to them. Pair of porcelain collies on the sill, cuckoo clock over the hutch, wool blanket we used to spread on the grass in the orchard, and who am I to turn any of these things away now? Am half surprised no ghost of Bob comes knocking on the window to let him in.

Or so I say to the kitchen. And the walls, the stove, the whole house holds so still it begins to shiver—that high-pitched hum of glassware in the quiet—and what a strange old shipwreck of a life this is, isn't it? Everything from Bayside to Greenpoint to the farm, all these bits and pieces trailing behind like so much debris. Doily my mother made, an old piece of sea glass, cupboard gnawed by a pet raccoon, and what's it all mean in the end?

Can stare the entire night at the light fixture on the ceiling, but that frosted glass, those dead shadows of bugs, none of it's going to help explain anything. The plates, the refrigerator, the sink and faucet, the entire room just wishing the lights were off. The cabinets and doorway trying to will me upstairs and into bed already. The curtains wavering slightly, saying, Get some rest, old woman… Wake up and see how you feel in the morning… Then go back to the farm if you want… Wear that nice skirt and blouse you've been saving… Shock the bejeezus out of whoever's left…

All right, I say to the house—and the rest of the night has me just tossing and turning, sheets and pillow hot to the touch—moonlight on the trees, shush of leaves in the dark, and over and over in my mind to the farm I go. Keep pulling up to the old house, keep standing in the yard, keep wondering who'll step onto the porch when I arrive—Danny, Margaret, Annie—and I must fall asleep somewhere in all of this, because the next thing I know is sunshine and that sharp green of trees outside. Whatever dreams I had, they disappear at the slightest touch, leaving me tired again, exhausted and heavy, as if I've covered some great distance in the night.

Beautiful day out there—and I get dressed, fix my hair, and start driving to the farm—stop for coffee, stop for gas, and one cool hour of highway to the exit and back roads again. Am forever on the verge of lost as I go—feel I'm trying to catch that dream again, trying to remember some story I read or heard a long time ago—the little church, the truss bridge, the old mills and towns to pass, everything familiar, everything strange, all of it leading to this fork onto Pautipaug Hill, and that déjà vu of cemetery in the gully, and then Bob's stone near the front gate as real as anything else in my life. Can see him gray and shining from half a mile away, like he's been watching all this time for me to pull up.

Robert S. Cussler
1926-1981

And I get out of the car—why not?—I hearby give myself permission to take this little detour of standing for who knows how long over my old husband like this. Just grass and sky and trees and birds and sunlight and air, and it's days, it's years, it's an entire lifetime before the sound of tires on gravel brings me back to the world, the pop and crackle of a pickup truck easing behind, and where am I now as I turn and straighten my skirt. Click of door opening, crunch of boots, and this man asking if that's really who he thinks it is.

I stand there—curious to know who I might actually be to him—and he opens his arms and says, Aunt Anna! It's me, Little Leo! Margaret and Leo's son!

To which I say, *That cannot be.*

He laughs in a way that makes me smile and puts his hand to show how tall he must have been last time I saw him—and he hugs me with those easy thick arms of his, old smell of hayloft and cows and kerosene—and then he holds me away, this man asking does anyone know I'm here?

I shake my head—can't seem to speak—Little Leo still this skinny little kid in my mind, his voice still squeaky and sweet as a girl's, that boy inside this disguise of a man somehow. He's saying to come to the farm, saying he'll call Uncle Danny and Aunt Annie, saying he'll see me up at the house, yes? He says all kinds of things that I can't really hear, all of which ends with him telling me to take my time with Uncle Bob.

And after he drives away, sound of his truck tapering up the hill, I turn and ask Bob if I should just go home. He's under the grass, my husband, but I see him smirk. What, exactly, he asks, is *home* again?

Oh, it's true, I say, even dead you have to be my nemesis, don't you?

When Bob doesn't say anything next to this, I spit his name and dates to the grass like watermelon seeds. Half of me feels bad for doing this, wants to take it back and say sorry, say I miss him and love him and all that girl gush—things I feel but never say—but the other half of me just scoffs, raises my face to the sun, takes a deep breath, and starts to the farm.

Up the hill and nothing seems to have changed. The barn, the main house, the cows, the junk trucks in the pasture. The orchard's a bit shaggier than I remember, but the hills, the fields, the light feels the same. Leo steps out of the house—and again that brush of sun and leaves, as if the world's saying everything's going to be all right—Leo's wife and daughter lovely and smiling beside him, five or six dogs wagging their way across the yard, all of us buoyed into the house, that candy-shop smell of hallway and kitchen, counters and sink the same celery green, table in the same place at the windows, brass lamp hanging same as ever from the ceiling.

Bob's brother Danny is on his way, says Leo, and just then Margaret and Ellen and Robert and April arrive together, and all the shotgun questions and jokes begin of how many years has it been? Ten? Twenty? Thirty years gone by? Tell me how does that happen? Honestly, just *how does that happen?*

No one seems to know—though it sure does happen, we say, doesn't it?—and we look at one another in disbelief, last time together being Bob's funeral, Bob's couch sitting in the next room, cushions frowning as if he might have died there just yesterday, pulmonary embolism, bowl of ice cream.

Still no Danny, and we wait and catch one another up on kids and grandkids and bouts with gout, gallbladder operations, and there's the sound of cutlery and ice in glasses as Bob's sister Annie shows up at the door. Leo helps her into the room, her back stooped as she crosses the kitchen, this old woman so much smaller than I remember. It's like hugging a bird cage, all wire and wicker in my arms, two of us trying not to cry as we look at each other, both of us gray and featherless by now, whiskers on her chin, and whiskers I know on mine.

Still no Danny, and Leo sets kielbasa and bread on the table, his wife bringing whiskey and beer and ice and more glasses, everyone drinking to old times and loved ones and how in a flash it all goes by.

Danny arrives, finally, appears like an older version of his brother—has to be a grand entrance, of course, that pull of stomach once more, as if Bob himself drifts into the room for a moment, nose battered, hair thin, same yellow sweepstakes smile of his, like he's just won a thousand dollars. We all hurrah for Danny, and soon I'm telling about these eels in the supermarket yesterday—*whole tank filled with eels*—which makes us remember the eel in my bathtub, which brings back the time Bob teaches me to drive, me going straight over the embankment, two of us upside-down in the car, windows blown-out, slushy sound of glass everywhere, and Bob looking at me, saying that I'm trying to kill him, aren't I? And I'm like, You idiot, why would I try to kill you in the same car *I'm* driving? We're on the ceiling together, hazards blinking, and he goes, I don't know, Anna, but I'm sure you have your reasons.

Danny seems to recall some drinking that afternoon, cider always in the cellar those days, Bob always offering to fetch the next pitcher. Even as a kid he'd be downstairs longer and longer, coming back all dizzy in the head, skinny little boy talking nonsense, sneaking out to sleep with the chickens in the coop.

We laugh—and everything rhymes with everything else—all of us remembering kids up in trees, a rabid coyote to shoot, Bob driving up to the farm the night of the flood, telling us not to worry, put all our important papers on top of the fridge. And in the morning? You guessed it—whole house gone, swept away, nothing but river—and we stand on the road, Bob rubbing the bristle of his chin. *Well,* he says, *there goes that.*

Didn't laugh so much back then, but we sure do laugh now. Entire afternoon we smile away like this, cheeks sore, and still nothing wrong with one last toast for old times' sake, is there?

Had our day, says Danny, didn't we?

Yes, we did.

Almost dark as we near the end of this, all of us around the table as the spell slowly lifts. And before anything else can happen, we have all these good nights on the porch to survive, all these hugs and kisses on the lawn to live through. Everyone walks me from the house to my car, the orchard and hills dark against the sky, dogs like shadows at our feet.

Leo says to come back anytime, always welcome. There's that verge of tears once more, mouth folding down with emotion, and here we go—this is what breaks my heart—Annie holding my hand in the dark, Danny touching my shoulder, me saying take care, all of us saying goodbye.

Back down the hill again, air plush and soft in the dusk, car heading toward the smell of river and that old gone house of ours. I idle slow where I feel our driveway must have been, place overgrown with vines and trees, water glassy black in the spaces below. Full dark by now, and I pull into what used to be our yard, everything quiet as I stand there. Sky nothing but stars. No moon, no clouds, just so many stars. A truck approaches and passes on the road, everything dark and quiet again. I lift my skirt and pee into the leaves, sound of steam escaping, wipe with the hem. And how incredible—all the stars, all the trees, all the water moving in the river—so dark and quiet as I lean on the warm car for who knows how long. End up driving lost until the middle of the night on these roads. And I'm just so grateful—am just so grateful and happy and tired and amazed—such an incredible sense of gratitude when I make it home at last.

Previously Published: The Architect of Flowers, Mariner Books, 2011.

Crazy Aunt Ruth's Legacy

James Magner

The mid-June late afternoon was pleasant enough in Western Illinois. But Tim was tired of waiting in the car parked across the street from the small Catholic church. Mollie always wanted to go to four pm Saturday Mass, which messed up the weekend a bit as far as he was concerned. Tim checked his phone for the time – 4:45, so the congregation should start exiting soon. He flipped the radio from the Rock station back to the Country station. Both had a lot of commercials, which made him even more impatient.

Finally, some action. A young mother and two small children burst out of the church door. She was clearly ready to depart as soon as it was respectable. Then several middle aged people stepped out, followed by an old lady using a walker who detoured right to descend on the ramp. Come on, Mollie!

There she was. Blue jeans and an attractive summer blouse. He liked the way her long dark hair fell around her shoulders. And the bounce of her breasts as step by step she descended the five stone stairs in front of the church door. She was a very good looking girl, he had to admit. And the love of his life. She was a year younger at twenty-three. And very Catholic. Luckily that didn't stop her from moving in with him. She said it was okay because they were truly in love and engaged. Tim, an unenthusiastic Protestant, had never been religious and had rarely attended services. If she wanted to be an active Catholic that was fine with him.

Tim was unconvinced about Divine Providence. During the four years that he studied at a small liberal arts college – he did get a business-related degree – first his father and then his mother died from cancer. And Mollie's parents were also dead. Since neither had a sibling, they were finding their way in the world themselves and saw the many advantages of teaming up. They were truly in love, yes, but their genuine partnership had many practical advantages as well.

Molly climbed into the front seat and leaned over to give Tim a warm, wet kiss.

"So, did you pray for me?"

"Of course, even though we both know there's no hope for a guy who only thinks about sex!"

"What? I also work for a living!"

"And that is much appreciated. So, Mr. Moneyman. I'm starving. Let's grab a burger." They always had fast food somewhere along the strip after mass.

Money was tight. Mollie worked as an assistant in a hair salon, and she really enjoyed the interactions with her small-town customers. For the past year Tim was an account manager at an office supply company. He liked his boss. Tim made a point of always being at his desk early and he avoided making any trouble. The paycheck was small but he and Mollie really needed the income.

"Anything interesting at mass?"

"Well, the Old Testament reading was about Jericho."

Tim pulled away from the curb. "Who was Jericho?"

Mollie laughed. "Silly! Jericho was a place. An old city with a big wall around it to keep out bad guys."

Tim gave Molly a quick blank stare, but he had to keep looking forward for traffic.

"Yeah, Joshua led the Israelites toward Jericho but they didn't know how to get inside the wall. So Joshua had the people blow trumpets and shout and the wall suddenly fell down. End of story. The Israelites took the city."

"Impressive. Must have been some pretty loud trumpets."

"It's a metaphor."

"What?"

"It's a story that has a deeper religious meaning."

"Meaning what?"

"Well, when you face an impossible challenge while trying to do something important, you prepare and do your best, but you also trust in God, and if it is His will He can make unlikely things happen to help you."

The weekend routine was interrupted Sunday at 2 pm by the phone call from Bill Edwards. He lived a block south of downtown Quincy next to Great Aunt Ruth, and accepted small payments to cut her grass and shovel her snow. He went next door at noontime to say hi like he did every Sunday, and he found her dead in the easy chair in the living room, the TV still on. Poor Ruth. She had been apparently pretty healthy for 96, but she refused to see doctors and something obviously caught up with her. Bill called the police and the body had just been taken to the funeral home on Broadway.

Tim had last seen her just two Sundays ago. He and Mollie visited her about one Sunday afternoon each month. But they were not close. Ruth was a very strong-willed and independent woman who appreciated that Tim did little chores for her from time to time. But she maintained her distance.

Only six mourners came to the funeral. Great Aunt Ruth had outlived nearly all of her relatives and friends. She was childless and Great Uncle Jack had died decades before. A skilled carpenter, he had earned a comfortable living doing construction, and he also made quality furniture and kitchen cabinets. So Jack and Ruth had been fairly well off for many decades. When Jack's short obituary appeared in the newspaper it drew little notice except by an unscrupulous Bible salesman who knocked on Ruth's front screen door three days later. He said he was there to deliver the gold-leaf deluxe Bible that Jack had ordered the prior month, and for convenience he could collect the $82 cost while he was there. Without missing a beat, Ruth instantly responded that it was unlike Jack to order an expensive Bible, but he would be home from work at 5:30 pm and the salesman could discuss it with him at that time. The salesman made a hasty retreat and never came back, but that encounter became an oft-repeated piece of family folklore.

Tim frequently mentioned Ruth to Mollie as "Crazy" Aunt Ruth because of her many idiosyncrasies, but that was mostly a term of endearment. She was a hardworking and thrifty woman who had been a child during the depression years of the 1930s. She was uneducated but naturally quite bright. She thought doctors were too expensive, and that banks could not be trusted. Her parents and grandparents lost their savings in 1931 despite being held by reputable banks, and that made a lasting impression on Ruth. It was understood that she kept cash at home, but this was little discussed. Tim recalled that Ruth had given him a shiny 1901 silver dollar on his 16th birthday, but on other birthdays and holidays her small gifts were mundane. When Tim was twelve he was surprised and impressed when he learned that she liked spy programs and apparently on occasion read a spy novel.

Now Ruth's only surviving relative was her great-nephew, Tim. And he was to see a local attorney, Mr. McCarthy, today about Ruth's will. Tim was a little nervous because he had never before met with an attorney, but he feigned confidence as he took a chair across the desk from the bespectacled, greying professional. The will was simple and brief. Tim, the executor, inherited her tiny house and her belongings, and her two financial assets: a checking account with $2000, and a savings account with $6000. Tim was not surprised that he was the sole heir, but he was rather shocked by the small amounts in the accounts. How could she have been surviving with very little money? The fact that she lived near the center of the small town and had a small grocery store, a bank, and a post office just a few steps from her front door apparently eased her ability to run simple errands on foot.

The attorney pointed out the one puzzling paragraph in the will, which was addressed to Tim personally. Tim was to do his best to remain a reverent Christian, and it was imperative that he allow Moses and Joshua to guide him to the land of milk and honey. The attorney offered no interpretation, but he did advise that in his opinion the small somewhat dilapidated house should be sold "as is" as soon as possible since the taxes and ongoing expenses would cause substantial costs month by month. The funeral expenses could be paid from the bank accounts. The probate process would be easily completed within a few weeks at a cost of about $1000, and all would be well. Tim thanked Mr. McCarthy, shook his hand, stuck his photocopy of the will in his jeans pocket, and drove home to tell Mollie all about it. She was smart and would have some opinions.

Mollie was aghast.

"It sounds like we need to sell that old house pretty quick or it will bankrupt us!" She took a breath and motioned for Tim to sit beside her at the kitchen table. "But let's think about this. What are our options?"

"Well, it would cost a fortune to make the house livable for us, and we just can't put that kind of money into that place. But I worry about selling quickly."

"Why?"

Tim lowered his voice and locked gazes with Mollie. "Some of us had thought that Ruth was hiding cash at home. We need time to look around before we just sell the place."

"Hiding cash….?" Mollie took a few more seconds to process the idea, then smiled. "Well, it's 2 pm. Why not go look right now?"

The key turned easily in the front door, and Tim and Mollie stepped into the small, well-worn living room. The rug was stained and ragged, and some of the stuffing was coming out of seams in the couch and the easy chair. They knew the small color TV worked so they would not have to test that – but they were reminded that the cable bill would be an ongoing expense and they should cancel first thing tomorrow.

Ruth's large purse was on the TV tray next to the easy chair, and it contained $115 in a tattered wallet. This was a great start, but they wondered what else might be in the house.

They walked through the kitchen and opened each drawer and cabinet, but all seemed routine. The single bedroom had a small chest of drawers, and they emptied each drawer onto the bed. Just old clothes and some toiletries. A quick search of the bathroom was unproductive. Tim stood in the hall and pulled down the attic access door that included a small wooden ladder to be unfolded. The attic light worked and Tim spent 15 minutes carefully stepping this way and that to look for a box or suitcase, but the attic was empty. There was no basement, so they stepped outside and lifted the door to the single-car garage. Ruth did not have a car, but along the walls of the garage were a dozen boxes of old household goods and an ancient gasoline-powered lawn mower that likely hadn't been started in 20 years. The garage was attached to the house and was set on a single concrete slab. There was a chest-high standard window looking out to the side-yard, and a quite small rectangular window high up on the back wall, presumably not to be opened but just to let in daylight.

A bit disheartened, Tim motioned for Mollie to sit in the easy chair as he collapsed onto the living room couch. "What do you think, Mollie?"

Mollie gazed first at one piece of furniture then another. "There's not that much stuff in this house, but I would say that a 'preliminary search' is negative – as might have been expected. Ruth was smart enough that if she was hiding money here, it probably could not be found just by looking for one hour."

"So. What next?"

"Let's tip over every piece of furniture to look at the bottom, or at least use a flashlight and mirror to look at the bottoms of things. There could be an envelope taped onto the bottom of something."

Tim retrieved his powerful flashlight from the glove compartment and they spent the next hour in that systematic search – to no avail.

Tired and flustered, they decided to go home and have dinner. As they departed they took a few items from the kitchen home with them.

They felt better after having something to eat, but were worried. They had looked pretty thoroughly. Perhaps there actually was no hidden cash.

After dinner the TV remained off and they continued discussing possibilities. Tim decided that he would speak with his boss in the morning and take one more day off from work – he wanted to focus on the search.

"You know," Mollie began. "There was that odd paragraph in the will addressed to you about Moses."

Bill pulled the photocopy from his pants pocket and read the sentence. "… Remain a reverent Christian, and it is imperative to allow Moses and Joshua to guide you to the land of milk and honey."

"That might mean something," proposed Mollie. "I think your Great Aunt didn't trust the lawyer so she left an obscure message for you. We can at least hope that she meant something important by that."

Tim remained doubtful, but he appreciated Mollie's attempt to help. His enthusiasm had waned and he only responded to her with a nod.

"And remember, there was a large Bible on the dresser in the bedroom. We should take a look at that tomorrow, especially at the pages that say something about Moses."

June 28 promised to be hot and sunny. They had coffee and cereal, and Tim was cleared by his boss to take another day off.

The key turned easily in the front door again. Mollie retrieved the Bible and they sat side-by-side on the living room couch to take a look. There were no notes written on the inside front or back covers, and apparently no marginal notes on any page. Not very promising. Being more familiar with the book than was Tim, Mollie slid the Bible onto her lap and looked through the early sections where Moses was mentioned, followed by mention of Joshua. But nothing was marked or stood out.

Mollie sat in silence. This had probably been a wild goose chase.

Tim also was rather flustered. He stood and stretched to relieve tension. As he stood in the center of the small room to face Mollie, his eye caught the 8 x 10 framed picture hanging on the wall above the couch. It depicted a prominent bearded man in a flowing robe, and other men presenting him with a wealth of produce – grapes and figs.

Tim lifted the picture off the hook on which it was hung and turned it so Mollie, who was still seated, could see. "So, Mollie," he laughed. "Is one of these guys Moses?"

Mollie held the framed picture in two hands and stared at it for what seemed a full minute before responding. "I'm not sure."

Tim stepped into the kitchen to grab a pliers and screw driver from the drawer. "Let's open it up and see if it contains a secret note!" He was joking, but he actually was hoping that there might be a letter inside.

Tim quickly bent the four metal prongs on the frame, lifted out the back cardboard, and then lifted out a white thin spacer piece of cardboard just behind the print. He tossed that spacer to the side. He carefully lifted out the picture itself and read aloud two words printed along the bottom, apparently placed there by the manufacturer. The words were a name: Giovanni Lanfranco. Tim looked at Mollie for any reaction. She looked puzzled but was reaching for her phone. After a quick search of the name she smiled and held up her phone so Tim could see.

"Lanfranco was the artist, and here is our painting. And here's the title: Moses and the Messengers from Canaan."

Tim felt a weak flutter of hope. He and Mollie inspected both sides of the picture carefully, and held it up to the window glass to look through the print. After ten minutes their hopes began to fade. There was nothing on the print to tie it to Ruth or to the house. But it was Moses.

"Hand me the frame," ordered Mollie. Tim handed it to her and she turned it this way and that looking for any small words written along the edges, but there was nothing.

"And the back cardboard."

Mollie again conducted a withering inspection, but there was nothing suspicious.

"Wasn't there also a piece of white cardboard?"

"The spacer," answered Tim. He retrieved that from the floor and Mollie turned it in her hands.

After a second Mollie sat up straight, and looked with wide eyes at Tim.

"What is it?" he asked.

"There are words written with an ink pen here, and there are five small rectangular holes cut into this cardboard."

"Let me see." Tim held the cardboard by the window and read the sentence. "…Give me a sure sign, 13 and save alive my father." Tim handed the cardboard back to Mollie.

Mollie mumbled, "There are four quite small rectangular holes cut near the left top of the cardboard, and the words are written below those holes. And there is a larger rectangular hole cut on the right top part of the cardboard. The height of that cut is the same as the other holes, but it is much longer horizontally."

Tim's mind was racing. He had seen something like this somewhere before, maybe on TV. It was a show about the Civil War. Spies, that's it! Civil War spies. Tim smiled, "I think I know what this is. It's a mask."

"A mask?"

"Yes. You place this cardboard mask over a written document or page in a book and certain letters and words show through revealing a secret message!"

"Progress!" Mollie exclaimed. But after a moment she frowned. "But what document or book page should we place the mask on?"

"Do the words mean anything to you?"

Mollie paused and furrowed her brow. "It is very odd to say this. But those words are vaguely familiar. I think I have heard something like this before. But I can't say when or where."

Tim crossed his fingers. "Please think, Mollie."

After a moment she smiled. "Better than thinking, I can just search that word phrase placed in quotation marks. If the phrase is widely known the source will pop up." Mollie grabbed her phone and entered the required text in quotation marks.

Mollie read the search result to Tim. "It's the end of verse 12 and the beginning of verse 13 of Joshua chapter 2. And that explains what the little superscript 13 is doing in the text."

Tim sat by Mollie's side and excitedly pointed at the Bible, which was still on her lap.

Mollie opened to the correct page of the Book of Joshua and placed the mask over the text. The four holes to the left side of the cardboard each allowed only one or two letters to be seen. That part of the message was derived from the underlined letters in the text that follows: "…Give me a sure sign, 13 and save alive my father…" and Tim quickly pointed out that the letters showing through spelled "silver." His pulse quickened.

Without delay, Mollie read the words that appeared through the larger rectangular slit on the right side: "…The scarlet cord in the window…"

Then Mollie added with a smile, "This is from the story of Joshua's siege of Jericho. That is where I had heard the phrase. At mass. The scarlet cord was the sign left in the window of the prostitute, Rahab, who helped the Israelite spies enter the walled city."

Tim was so excited he could hardly speak. "And I think I know where there is a scarlet cord. It is in the high rectangular window in the back wall of the garage."

They rushed to the garage, and Tim slid several heavy boxes full of junk away from the back wall. The scarlet cord was thumbtacked to drape across the top of the window and hung down both sides as far as the sill. It looked like the sorry remnant of what once had been red curtains that had covered the window, but now only the cord remained. Tim carefully inspected the wall from the concrete floor up to head height, but there was no access panel. They briefly walked outside but the exterior of the wall also had no obvious access. It was a quite solidly built wooden wall that didn't jiggle at all, and it was firmly set on the concrete floor.

Back inside the garage, Mollie pointed upward toward four small horizontal dark stripes on the back wall. Located about six feet above the floor, and just below the level of the high window sill, each stripe was about four inches long horizontally and only a fraction of an inch high vertically. The four marks were spread at about 3 foot intervals across the back wall. Tim reached up and easily felt the marks.

"They're not stripes," he reported. He turned and grabbed Mollie's hands, and the moment was electric. "They're slits."

Tim grabbed a large hammer and crowbar from the junk pile in the corner, paused, and held up the tools as he locked gazes with Mollie. His gesture was asking for Mollie's approval to proceed with some demolition.

She nodded. Then she added with a grin, "Shall I blow a trumpet?"

The wall had been solidly built, but within minutes a two foot hole was clawed out at the base. And out poured thousands – no, tens of thousands – of silver dollars.

Ante Meridiem

Bill Mesce, Jr.

THE GREYHOUND BUS waddled off and around the corner on its bad shocks, leaving him coughing and batting at a blue cloud of fumes. His lungs cleared and the echoes of grinding gears faded. He studied the wake of exhaust lingering in the street, watched it rise into the fluorescence of the street lamps, thin, and finally disappear.

He put his duffel bag down in front of the station's open door and walked across the parking apron to the curb. Downtown was dark buildings, dark store windows, dark theater marquees. The street was wide, lined with red-flagged parking meters, and filled with a humid, sticky haze that lit up in fuzzy haloes around the buzzing street lights.

He shrugged off his denim jacket and plucked at where his shirt was already adhering to him. He bent for the duffel and went inside.

A weeping willow of a kid sat on a stool behind the counter, thumbing through an issue of *Maxim*. The kid did not look up at the sound of footsteps, and he did not look up when the man stood at the counter. The kid did not look up when the man raised his duffel and let it drop to the linoleum floor with a loud, flat slap.

"Hey," the man said.

He was eighteen, maybe nineteen, and rested a hand protectively around the base of the bottle of Dr. Pepper sitting next to *Maxim*. He twirled a long lock of stringy, greasy hair with his other hand.

"Hey."

The kid looked up. His nose twitched and he leaned back from the counter. The man could smell it himself; he'd been on the bus a long time.

The man leaned forward. "Connection to New York."

The kid leaned back another degree and waited for more.

"When?"

The kid nervously rubbed one of several nasty-looking red splotches along his collar line. "When's it comin'?" he said in a slow, rural drip.

"Yeah."

The kid checked a schedule taped to the counter top. "Five thirty."

"Five thirty? A.M.?"

The kid had gone back to his magazine. "If he's on time. Sometimes he ain't on time."

"Is he late a lot?"

"Nope."

The man took a long, patient breath. "Five thirty. A.M. If he's on time. And he's not late a lot."

"Yup."

"Thanks so much. No, really, thank you."

He picked up his duffel bag with a grunt and shuffled past the counter to the empty waiting room. The Dr. Pepper clock high on one wall said it was three thirty-six. A.M.

The man moaned.

He dropped his bag on one of the Day-Glo orange plastic chairs and ran his jacket through the bag's grips. There was a bank of dark vending machines along one wall. He dropped some change into a soda machine. He stared at the machine. The machine stared back. The man jiggled the coin return but nothing happened.

"Hey!" he called to the kid. "This thing ate my money."

The kid flipped a page of *Maxim*.

"Hey!"

The kid looked up and blinked, confused.

The man tapped on the soda machine. "My money."

"That thing ain't on. Couldn't you tell?"

"How 'bout my money?"

"They unplug 'em at night."

"What do they unplug 'em for?"

The kid shrugged.

"What am I supposed to do 'bout my money?"

"Day fella's got the keys. Don't come in 'till seven-thirty."

"If he's on time."

"What?"

"Forget it." He thought about asking the kid where he'd gotten *his* soda, but the heat, the humidity, the dead soda machine and the conversation exchanged thus far were all giving him a headache.

He sat in the chair next to his bag. He sagged and let his head loll onto the curled top of the chair back. He drummed absently on his legs. He managed a few good rhythmic licks and wondered if he should've taken drum lessons when he was a kid. He carefully balanced the heel of one worn sneaker on the toe of the other. He looked up at the clock again.

It was three thirty-eight. A.M.

He moaned.

He stood up, stretched, and headed for the men's room. At the door he stopped and looked from the kid picking at a pimple scab on his forehead to his duffel bag. He went back, grabbed the bag and took it with him into the men's room.

He had to wrestle with the bag for space just to make enough room to get the door closed; the bathroom wasn't much bigger than the closet-sized toilet on the bus. He set the bag down on the grungy tile and kept tripping over it while he peed, then washed his hands at the sink. He threw some cold water on his face. It helped ease the ache in his head and the burning in his eyes.

The face in the mirror made him moan again. He scratched the whiskered neck and touched tentatively at the gray strands at his temple. He stepped as far back as the little room allowed, stood up straight, in profile, checking his figure in the mirror. He sucked in his belly. Wouldn't look too bad as long as he never breathed.

He used his hands as a cup to rinse his mouth out with the metallic-tasting water from the tap, then turned to the linen tower dispenser and tugged for a stretch of fresh towel. The dispenser didn't have any more clean linen to dispense. Gingerly, he patted his hands on the clammy part of the towel hanging exposed and hoped he wouldn't catch anything.

Back in the waiting room, the clock now read three forty-three. A.M.

He moaned.

He dropped back into his chair and listened to the kid flip magazine pages. He fished in his breast pocket and pulled out an empty pack of gum. He crumpled the foil pack and, after looking to see the kid's attention was still in his magazine, tried to hook-shot the wad into a trash can across the room. He missed.

The man looked over to the kid to make sure the kid wasn't looking.

The kid was looking.

The man flashed a brief, insincere smile of apology to the kid while he grunted himself to his feet and placed the crumpled pack in the trash can. He gave the kid another empty smile, an acknowledgment of his act of atonement, and the kid went back to his magazine, and the man back to his chair.

"Hey."

The man jumped. He hadn't seen the bum slip into the seat next to him. He guessed the bum was old but under the dirt and beard and ragged clothes it was hard to tell. The bum probably smelled, too, but the man smelled so badly himself he couldn't be sure.

The bum smiled. There weren't a lot of teeth in there.

The man picked up his duffel and shifted to the next seat over. He looked away, pretending to find something to study in a cobwebbed corner of the ceiling.

"Hey," the bum said.

"What?"

"Waitin' on a bus?"

The man closed his eyes and tried to wish the bum away.

The bum moved into the seat next to him. He pointed to the shoulder patch on the man's jacket jammed through the duffel's hand grips; a diving bald eagle on a black background.

"Hunnerd 'n' First!" the bum said, impressed. "Screamin' Eagles, yessir! You inna Hunnerd 'n' First?"

"No."

"You inna service?"

"No."

"Vietnam?"

"I said I wasn't in the service."

"Too young for Nam. 'At Gulf thing. The firs' one."

"I said I wasn't in the service," and this time he said it slowly and carefully.

The old man was studying him through narrowed, rheumy eyes. "Yeah, you woulda been too young. So, wheredja get it?" He tapped the patch with the flapping sole of an unraveling canvas sneaker.

The man hooked his own foot around his bag and pulled it a distance from the bum. "It was a gift."

"Somebody give ya *that* as a gift? 'At's some kinda weird – "

"Then it wasn't a gift, ok?"

"Somebody ya know give it to ya?"

"Somebody I knew."

"Like who?"

"You with the census or somethin'?"

The bum smiled and shrugged as if that was explanation enough.

The man sighed. "Like my old man."

The bum nodded and looked away, seemingly satisfied for the moment.

They sat like that for a while, taking turns sighing with boredom.

Then the bum said, "Yeeeeaaaahhh, I was inna Hunnerd 'n' First, dontcha know."

"I didn't know."

"Yup. Good ol' Hunnerd 'n' First. I was with 'em in the big one. World War and Number Two."

"World War II."

"Good ol' boys, ever' one of 'em. The best. Battle of the Bulge, dontcha know."

"I don't have any money for you, pal, ok?"

"Battered Bastards of the Bastion of Bastogne," the bum said. "'At's what 'ey called us – "

The man leaned toward the bum and spoke slowly and carefully. "I don't have any money for you. And the Battle of the Bulge was over sixty years ago. You're lookin' pretty spry."

The bum faced him and smiled slowly, then laughed himself into a coughing fit so loud and violent even the kid at the counter looked up.

"Yer a smart boy, boy," the bum wheezed when the fit subsided. "Yer ok."

"Thanks."

After a while, the bum had his wind back and the two of them sat silently in the bright plastic chairs for a few seconds. The man slouched down and put one hand over his eyes but he couldn't sleep.

"I really *was* inna Hunnerd 'n' First, dontcha know," the bum said. "Korea. But you say Korea and nobody knows what yer talkin' 'bout. Yup, the ol' *Pooo-san* Perimeter. Betcher daddy wan' even born – "

The man sat up. "You settle for a cigarette?"

"Hell, sure!"

The man fished a squashed pack of Kents out of his hip pocket. He drew two bent, leaking cigarettes, took one for himself and handed the other to the bum, then lit them both.

"Yer ok, boy," the bum said.

"You finished now?"

The bum looked offended, gave a conceding smile and nodded. "I'm done."

"Then goodnight."

The bum nodded a thanks for the cigarette and shuffled out.

"Hey!"

It was the kid. He was pointing to a sign reading, "THIS AREA IS

SMOKE FREE."

The man pulled himself out of his chair and squashed the cigarette out on the side of the trash can across the room before tossing the butt out. He looked up at the clock and moaned: it was going on three forty-eight. A.M.

He walked to the kid at the counter. "Hey, there some all-night place I can maybe get something to eat? A coffee or a soda or somethin'?"

The kid didn't look up. The man craned his head around to see what was holding the kid's attention. He saw a picture of some young thing he vaguely remembered from TV. She was standing in the surf wearing bikini bottoms and a man's white dress shirt, unbuttoned and nicely and transparently plastered to her form by sea spray. The man didn't remember her looking that shapely on TV, but then on TV she was usually dressed.

"Over to Main Street," the kid said.

"Hm?" The man pulled his head back into place.

"Main Street."

"Where's that?"

"A block over," the kid nodded, "hang a left. Just keep goin' 'till ya see it."

"Is it far?"

The kid shrugged.

The man hefted up his bag and headed outside.

He didn't like the streets. Mannequins stood embalmed in half-lit store windows. Above the stores were dark windows of empty offices and quiet apartments. No night lights. Not even a night owl's blue glow of a TV. Air conditioners hummed, fans whirred, the street lamps buzzed, but the street was still dead and he didn't like that.

There were alleys and they were dark, too. Things scampered along the ground deep inside the darkness and rattled the garbage cans.

"Great," the man said half aloud. He walked quickly and stared straight ahead. He didn't want to see what was making the noises.

He crossed on to Main Street. It was brighter, bigger, and deader except down at one end where he could see the lights of a little café.

Inside, it was small and dull with a tile floor like the men's room back at the bus station. There were a few booths along one wall and a counter down the other. There was a dark juke box at one end, still fans hanging from the ceiling, and an air conditioner over the door that dripped water on him as he stepped inside.

In a back booth, someone was slumped over the table. A black man in cook's whites puttered around in the kitchen. A bleached-blonde who looked like the woman in Maxim only plus twenty years and thirty pounds but trying not to look it was tucked into a waitress uniform with little room to spare. She was leaning on the counter reading a paperback and on the cover was a picture of a mustachioed man in Victorian tails, a woman in a hoop skirt, and they were waltzing under the title, *The Dastardly Duke*.

The man found a stool at the counter whose vinyl was not cross-hatched with patches of duct tape. He tucked his bag under his legs while the waitress swing-hipped her way over with a big smile of big teeth stained with candy red lipstick. Close up he could see she'd mistakenly thought she could shave off a few years by pancaking on the make-up. He marveled that all that plaster didn't crack when she opened her mouth. "Help ya, hon?" she asked.

"Coffee."

"Coffee."

"And an English muffin."

"English muffin?"

"Yeah."

She started writing out the check. "That it?"

"That's it."

"Want the coffee with the muffin?"

"I'll take it now."

She handed the check to the cook, then poured a cup from the Bunn-omatic behind the counter.

He got change of a dollar from her and went to the juke box, dropped in some change and looked up and down the accordioned title cards. He didn't see anything he liked but picked a few numbers anyway.

Nothing happened.

He started banging on the juke box.

"Hey!" the waitress warned.

"I lost my money."

"Thing ain't plugged in, hon. Can't you see?"

"Why didn't you say something when I asked for change? What'd you think I wanted it for?"

"Maybe you were gonna buy cigarettes or somethin'."

"You have a cigarette machine in here?" He made a show of looking around for the non-existent cigarette machine. "How 'bout my money?"

"Can't give it to you outta the register. They gotta get your money outta the machine."

"And the day fella's got the key, right?"

"What?"

"Can you just plug it in so I can get my money back?"

She made a face. "Not s'pose to do that."

"I promise I won't tell."

"Mister, how long you think I'm gonna keep this lousy job doin' things I'm not s'pose' to do?"

He held up his hands in surrender and went back to his stool. "You're right. I don't know what's the matter with me. I must be out of my mind or somethin'." He made himself calm down and took a sip of his coffee. He blinked. He guessed the coffee must've been sitting on the Bunn-omatic for hours. He took another sip. Maybe days.

"You come in on that last bus?" the waitress said. "They go right by here is how I know."

The man nodded.

She rang up "No Sale" on the cash register, took out some change and handed it to him. "For the juke. I figgered since you come in onna bus."

He missed the logic but smiled a thanks anyway.

"So," she said, "you from outta town?"

"Yeah."

"Back east, right?"

"Yup."

She smiled proudly at her deductive powers. "Where 'bouts?"

"Is that my muffin burning?"

"Kitchen always smells like that."

"Order up!" called the cook.

The waitress scooped up the muffin and set the little white plate down on the counter in front of him.

"Is it supposed to be that dark?" the man said frowning at the muffin.

"Better when it's crunchy like that. You gonna be in town long?"

He scraped at the charred edge of the bread. "No." He said it hard enough to send her off, slightly offended, to trade mumbles with the cook.

"Hello."

He hadn't heard the door, or her cross the floor and slide onto the stool next to him. She was small, young, and black. She was dressed well, a simple, short one-piece thing, and had a better flair for make-up than the waitress.

"You in on the bus?" she asked.

"People in this town are perceptive as hell."

"Waiting on another one?"

He nodded.

"Need a place to sack out for a few hours?"

"I am not a rich man."

"How do you know I'm just not the social type?"

"I guess I don't."

She tapped the shoulder patch on the jacket still tucked through the grips of his bag. "Let's just say I'm doing my bit."

He considered saying something about the patch but passed. He wrinkled his nose: "I've been on the bus a while."

"I've got a shower."

"Ok, then." He smiled and started to get up.

"No rush. Finish your food."

He offered her half his English muffin but she smiled and shook her head. He took a sip of the acrid coffee and a crunchy bite of the muffin. "I think I'm finished." He reached for his pocket but she stopped him.

"My treat," she said, reaching for her purse.

He thought about how thin his wallet was and decided against asserting his gallantry.

On the sidewalk, they walked side by side.

"Thanks," he said.

"For what?"

He nodded back at the café.

"Forget it. You, um, didn't mind, did you?"

"I'm a modern guy."

"You can put your arm around me if you want."

He did.

They came to a bank of dreary row houses. She started up the stoop of one of them, fumbling in her purse for her keys. He stayed at the foot of the stairs, taking in the gaunt, dark-eyed building.

"I know it isn't the Sheraton," she said.

He felt guilty and put on a smile. "Sheraton's uppity."

He followed her inside and up a stairway lit by bare bulbs to the third floor. The apartment was three rooms and a little bathroom. She headed for the bedroom.

"You coming?" she asked.

"Just getting my breath from all those damn stairs."

The bed had a noticeable sag down the middle. There was just the bed, one scuffed dresser, and a lamp on a night stand. She didn't turn on the lamp.

"Make yourself at home," she said, kicking off her shoes. "Drink?"

He shook his head and dropped his bag near the bedroom door.

"Hungry?"

He shook his head again.

"Anything the matter?"

Another shake of his head.

She slid out of her dress. She wasn't wearing anything underneath. Some street light slipped in under the half-pulled window shade. Wherever it touched her, her skin shone smooth and dark like freshly poured chocolate. He had a glimpse of slim thighs, a slight bulge of belly, dark, erect nipples.

She stood against him. Her head was just below his chin. She felt warm even through his clothes.

"Cat got your tongue?" she said and pulled his head down toward hers. She kissed him, open-mouthed, and nibbled when he sent his tongue out to meet hers.

"Now thee doeth," he said around his captured tongue and they both laughed.

He sat in the open window, looking out at the streets, a towel tied around his hips. Fresh from the shower, the air – humid as it was – felt good on his wet skin.

"Don't you sleep?" she asked.

"I did. For a while."

She stretched her arms overhead. He liked the way the movement tightened up her small breasts.

"Where you heading?" she asked.

"East."

"Where you from?"

"East."

"Ah. Going home."

He shrugged. He went to his jacket and pulled out his Kents. He offered the pack to her but she shook her head. He lit up, took a long drag, then parked himself back in the window, leaning against the sill, letting the smoke bleed out of his mouth.

"Been away long?" she asked.

He shrugged. "How long is long? You know..."

"What?"

He nodded at the jacket saddled across the top of his duffel. "That doesn't belong to me."

"The jacket?"

"The *jacket's* mine. The patch..."

"Oh."

"So much for you doing your bit. I guess I owe you one."

She shrugged it off. "Didn't really matter. It was something to say."

"Ah."

"Is that just your idea of decoration? That supposed to be cool? Or – "

"It was my father's." He took another long drag on his cigarette. "He didn't come home."

Her head lowered. "The Gulf?"

"Nope. He came home from *that*. He just didn't come *home*. They discharged him at Fort Campbell. That's in Kentucky. Gave him his papers, his mustering out pay... He mailed me a hundred bucks, that patch, and a note that said, 'Good luck, junior,' and that was that."

She nodded gravely. "Oh." She ran her fingers through her short, spongy hair. "Got anything lined up?"

He laughed self-mockingly, and ruffled his damp hair. "Hadn't really thought that far."

She lay back on the squeaking mattress. "Want to come back to bed? C'mon, you were nice."

"She said with well-rehearsed allure to the Dastardly Duke."

"I was serious," she said, hurt.

He looked back out the window. "Sorry."

"Come back to bed," she said. "Please."

He flicked the cigarette out the window. It made a long, glowing arc down to the sidewalk where it exploded in the shadow of the curb in a burst of orange sparkles. Like a falling star.

They walked down the street holding hands as if they'd known each other a long time. Over toward the east, the dark sky was starting to fade.

"You don't have to see me off," he said.

"I'll just walk you to the station."

"You don't have to."

"If I *had* to, I probably wouldn't."

They walked silently. He ran his thumb along the back of her hand.

"What would you do?" he asked after a while.

"About what?"

"If you were in my boat."

"I'm not."

"If you were."

"If I were, I think I'd find somebody better to ask advice from than mysterious women of dubious repute whom I meet in the middle of the night in the middle of nowhere."

"Like who?"

"If I knew, *I'd* be doing some advice-asking myself."

Outside the station doors she kissed him. Gently, sweetly. She let go his hand slowly, stepped back, then turned and walked back down the street.

He stood there watching her go until she disappeared around a corner. He went inside.

The kid was still there still picking pimples and still flipping through his magazine. "Find it ok?" the kid asked.

"Yeah."

"You were gone a long time."

The man shrugged. He looked at the clock. It was five-fifteen. A.M.

He started to sit in the waiting room but stopped. He headed for the door but stopped. He headed back for his chair but stopped.

The kid was looking at him trying to decipher the man's particular difficulty.

"Aw, hell," the man grumbled. He threw his bag on the counter by the kid. "Watch that."

"Hey!" the kid called after him.

The man ran outside and up to the corner where he thought the girl had disappeared.

"Hey!" he called out. The windows looking down on the street stayed dark and the store mannequins remained mute.

"Hey!"

He ran past a traffic light click-clicking changes over an empty Main Street. He looked up, then down toward the lights of the café.

"Hey!"

The side streets all looked the same...and they all looked unfamiliar.

He could hear the rumbling echo and hissing air breaks of the bus.

He jogged back to the station and grabbed his bag from the kid.

"She's gonna be two minutes late it looks like," the kid reported.

The man ignored him and took his bag with him out onto the parking apron.

The bus was three minutes late.

The door hissed open for him.

He didn't get in.

"Sure?" the driver said.

"Nope," the main sighed.

The driver closed the door and turned the bus back onto the street, leaving the man coughing and batting at a fresh cloud of blue fumes.

He shifted his bag to his other hand and headed up the street toward where the sky was growing light to see if he could find some place to stay.

Originally published in The Monongahela Review, Summer 2008 issue.
Reprinted in Precis, author's short story collection, published by Stephen F. Austin University Press, 2012.

Waiting on Angels

Colleen Kearney Rich

I follow the health care worker into my grandmother's room, where she calls in a loud melodious voice, "Look grandmother, it's granddaughter. She's come for a visit." She gestures as if she is presenting me. My grandmother smiles at me politely and looks away.

In a way, I do need an introduction. Although I see my grandmother every few weeks, it's been months since she has recognized me.

"Do I know you?" she asks each time and each time I tell her who I am and then stand still while she tries to recognize me.

"Whose child are you?" she always asks next.

"Your daughter Irene," I answer. "The one you live with."

She usually nods at this point, but there is always a pained expression on her face as if the news is somehow troublesome to her.

Today she is sitting in her recliner with a shawl over her legs. The shawl is ratty looking from too many washes and the straps of her slip hang down her arms past the sleeves of her housecoat. She has grown tinier with each passing year, giving the impression that she is disappearing into her clothes.

I sit in the chair across from her and concentrate on the charming things about the room that remain. The photos of all of us grandkids at various awkward stages of growing up, the Mother's Day cards stuck in the rim of the mirror over the dresser, the gold cross from her Golden Wedding anniversary. Jesus stares down at me from one wall, his palms open, his heart glowing red through his robe, wrapped in thorns. He beseeches me to rise to the occasion.

I ask my grandmother if I can get her anything and she just shakes her head. She is looking at the television sadly, not really watching.

"Do you still watch your shows?" I ask, trying to initiate a conversation, wanting to hear a voice, any voice, even my own. When I was small, we would watch soap operas together. *All My Children* was her favorite.

She looks at me a moment and shrugs.

"Remember *All My Children*, the one with Erica?" I offer but get no response.

We have always called my grandmother Babci, which is an anglicized version of the Polish word for grandmother. In her younger days, Babci was a short round woman, who always wore her hair rolled up in bobby pins and tucked up in a hairnet. She dressed in large, shapeless dresses and carried a huge, stiff purse with large snapping clasp.

"How about I make us some tea," I say.

"I don't have any money," she tells me.

"Do you need some?"

"I can't pay you for all this," she says gesturing to the room. "I know I've been here a long time. I could write my mother and ask her to send you some money."

"This is your room," I say, hoping to skirt any conversation regarding my dead great grandmother. "You live here. It is your tea I am going to make. You don't need money. If anything I should be the one paying you."

"Oh," she murmurs, almost pleased. "This is a nice place," she says looking around the room.

"I'm not telling her anything anymore," my mother warned me several months before. All this followed a day when my grandmother thought she was a young girl and was looking for her older brother. All of her siblings are gone—Stan, who died in his 30s, long gone.

"It doesn't matter anyway. If she asks about Stan, tell her he's at work, or he's not home yet."

When I can't find anything worth watching on TV, I pull out some old photo albums to amuse myself and show Babci pictures of weddings and summer vacations, photos from her golden wedding anniversary—some of the last photos taken of my grandfather before he died. She looks mildly interested, but there is no sign of recognition.

"My eyes are tired," she tells me. "I want to lay down."

I help her out of the chair and into the bed. Her skin is crepey, so thin that it is nearly transparent. Purplish bruises spot one of her forearms. They appear to be from banging her arm against the nightstand beside her bed. My hands sink into her flesh as I hold her arms, right through to her bones. I take off her glasses and gently fold them up.

"Here is the cup for your teeth," I say, and she shakes her head. "They are supposed to soak overnight."

She closes her eyes tight. "No," she says quietly but firmly and mumbles something in Polish. Her head sinks into the pillow, her gray hair baby fine and almost as transparent as her skin. I lift her legs over the side of the mattress and push them close to the wall.

"Okay?" I whisper.

"Okay," she mutters as I cut off the light.

I can hear her whispering to herself in Polish. Maybe she is praying.

Kay, the health care worker, is packing up her things when I come back into the kitchen.

"She said she wanted to go to bed," I tell her. "That's okay right?"

Kay chuckles. "Your grandmother naps on and off all day. That's fine."

I check the lists on the countertop. My mother has gone to great lengths to keep my grandmother at home. There are helpers like Kay and prescriptions and lists and appointments. I too am a helper. My mother is off to meet my older sister's newest baby, the third grandchild. I have offered to stay with my grandmother for the long weekend.

"You've got this," Kay tells me, and she sounds certain. I am not as certain.

I watch Kay get into her tiny car and drive away and count how many hours it will be until she returns in the morning.

I am staying in my old bedroom, which looks pretty much the same as I left it, a shrine to my high school years. Yes, this is a good thing, I think. I don't miss the cracked plaster of my apartment, the yellowed linoleum, or the roaches. I settle in under my old quilt and expect to feel safe. Instead I feel trapped.

My heart seems to be percolating. Three beats, a pause, then another beat, fluttering like a moth against my ribs. I go over and push open the window. It is a cold night, but I stand with my face against the screen for several minutes before I start to feel better.

I realize I am scared to death that Babci will die during one of these nights, and I will be the one to see her first. I will be the one responsible. I try to imagine what she would look like dead. Would her lips be blue? Would I know from the door or have to go over and find a pulse? I tiptoe down the hall and stand outside of her room. I can hear her breathing, soft and even.

Not tonight, I think, trying to strike a bargain with the Christ figure on the wall, not this week. Back in my bed I decide to try and pray, maybe that will make me feel better, but I only remember certain prayers, the easy ones like "Our Father" and "Hail Mary." I pray to God and the Virgin Mary to spare me before I can finally relax enough to sleep.

In the morning, I am practically waiting by the door for Kay. The whiteness of her pantsuit and shoes comforts me. She bustles into the house. The polyester of her uniform makes a swishing sound against her bulk as she walks, her rubber soles squeak along the floors with her energetic little steps, and it's almost musical. I give her my number at work and practically leap down the porch steps.

Now work is something I can handle. I work in the accounts payable department of a government consulting firm. There is no mystery here. The numbers add up or they don't. If they don't, you find the error. Simple. So at work I can forget for a little while. I drink coffee and call my friends.

As the clock ticks closer to five, my heart starts to flutter again and I try to come up with a game plan to get me through another night. By the time I reach the house, I feel a tremendous need to confess to Kay I'm not equipped for the job. I don't know CPR. I don't know anything.

I watch Kay move around my grandmother's room with such composure and efficiency that I'm too embarrassed to talk. Maybe there is something lacking in me. Maybe I really am as selfish as my sister has suggested. I watch Kay spoon some kind of soup into Babci and wipe the corners of her mouth. Kay jabbers away while she scrapes the spoon up the side of the bowl, telling us anecdotes about her children, her other patients. She is this total mother, an absolute nurturer, doing things for Babci that she would do for a baby, things my sister Denise probably does for her children, and she makes them all seem normal, perfectly ordinary.

I am thinking about this while I listen to her stories, and at some point I realize I may have found the key. By pretending it is perfectly normal, perfectly ordinary, she maintains the dignity of these old people. So I decide right then and there I have to convince myself this is ordinary, a part of life.

What would Denise do, I think. Denise is the kind of person who would help a stranger on the street. She would buy a homeless person breakfast. I've seen her do it. What would Denise do for Babci? She would focus on little things like giving her a manicure or setting her hair. So that night, after Kay leaves, I give her a manicure. I soak her wrinkled fingers, then file her nails and paint them a dusty rose color I find in the bathroom.

Taking my cue from Kay, I babble on endlessly about our previous history. I talk about the old neighborhood. I tell Babci about the cat she got for me from the grocer, how she used to let me pick out chickens at the butcher, about the family down the street from her who had ten kids.

"Do you remember how many loaves of bread and gallons of milk they had to buy a day?" I ask her.

"No," she replies simply as if she is keeping up with the conversation.

"I can't remember either, but I know it was a lot," I admit. "I could never remember the names of those kids either. But I think they had two sets of twins."

"Oh, yes," she murmurs in agreement while inspecting her nails, but there's no connection. I can't reach her. This is cocktail party talk, beauty parlor talk. I'm just some woman painting her nails.

While I'm in the bathroom down the hall putting away the nail polish, I hear her. She is having a lengthy conversation with someone, using longer sentences than I've heard her utter all year. My mother has warned me but I haven't believed it until I hear her myself. People have begun to visit Babci, people no one else can see. I stand outside her bedroom door listening as she holds a conversation with one of her invisible guests.

"No, please stay as long as you like," she says, "I really like it when you come to visit. I get so lonely sometimes." She pauses waiting for an answer.

"Come sit in this chair, next to me. We'll watch some TV." I lean against the door making it creak, and the conversation ceases. She knows someone is listening. When I enter the room, she is silent.

"Who were you talking to?" I ask and she tries to introduce me to the friend, a child, but the little girl won't talk to me.

"Tell the nice lady your name," she coaxes. "Tell her where you're from. It's okay."

I wait, straining to hear an answer. After a moment, Babci smiles at me apologetically.

At first Babci would just see people who weren't there. "Is that your husband?" she would ask my mother, startling her because my father lives a half a country away with his new wife and family. But these people, these ghosts, they are always the same—a man, some little girls, an old woman, a baby boy. My mother warned me that the visits were more frequent now.

I try to imagine these imaginary friends of Babci's as angels, and it becomes easier to relax somehow. I think about beautiful women in flowing gowns and graceful, gentle wings. Something makes me get out of bed and look for my old Catholic school things in my jewelry box. It is where I thought it would be—a scapular. When I was little my mother would place them between our box springs and mattresses. I guess it was to keep us safe. It seems like such an old fashioned Catholic thing to do, superstitious. I take out the little plastic, beribboned thing and place it under my mattress. And I think "trust," trust God, just trust.

I'm downstairs in the kitchen putting on some water for our nightly cup of tea when she calls, "Somebody help me."

I run all the way thinking she has spilled something on herself or fallen. Instead I find her sitting composed in the recliner, pointing.

"What is it?" I ask. "Can I get you something?"

"The boy. He really should be in bed," she says, gesturing to a corner of her bed. "Could you put him to bed for me?"

I look where she is pointing and around the room a moment before telling her there's no one there. She sighs and looks away, dismissing me.

By the time I get back to the kitchen, she calls out again. "Help me. Isn't there anyone here who can help me?"

"Couldn't you please put him to bed," she asks me, gesturing to the same spot on the bed. "Look, he's fallen asleep. Please help me. Can you carry him?"

I walk over to the place she has been pointing and scoop the child into my arms and carry him from the room. I walk down the hallway with the bundle in my arms. I carefully place the dream child onto the bed in the next room as the teapot starts to whistle.

Magic

Nancy Wick

I sat in the cluttered back room of Astrology et al, a genuine Seattle woo-woo store, waiting for Jeff's predictions about the New Year. He perched on a stool across a small table from me, some of his frizzy blond hair escaping his ponytail and floating about his face like the fluff of a milkweed blossom as he listened to me tell him what I wanted. This wasn't the first time I'd consulted a "fortune teller." I'd had my horoscope cast, my tarot cards read and my aura photographed. But that didn't mean I believed everything these people told me. Unlike Nancy Reagan, I wasn't planning my life around the position of the stars.

I was, however, trying to pay attention to the "Law of Attraction" I'd read about in books like *The Aquarian Conspiracy*. It said that you will attract into your life the things you place your attention on, so I'd repeated affirmations (statements of how I wanted my life to be), closed my eyes and conjured up visualizations (mental images of those goals) and put together treasure maps (collages depicting my desires, using words and pictures from magazines). None of it constituted magic, exactly; I was just trying to latch onto that mysterious guiding force in the universe they talked about in the *Star Wars* movies.

I told myself I took it all lightly, but deep down, I had to admit, I hoped the magicians' predictions might come true, the images I dreamed up become reality.

Jeff—who the year before had spelled out for me all the key points on my astrological chart—was wearing his usual faded blue jeans and a tie-dyed shirt, moving his long, lanky body as though he was walking through water. I always felt a little off balance when he looked at me, as if he could see more than I wanted him to, but then, it was that "second sight" of his that I was counting on. I needed to know what 1986 had in store for me.

Jeff spread out my chart, keyed some calculations into a computer behind him, and when the printer spit out a piece of paper, he studied it, making some notes. Then he looked up, his wide hazel eyes locking on mine. "You're about to meet your life mate," he said, "and soon, so you'd better get ready."

My body jerked back involuntarily and I sat up straighter, blinking at Jeff's placid face. His pronouncement was shockingly specific. The various purveyors of magic I'd consulted in the past tended to say things like "the time is favorable" for this or that. But there was no hedging in what he'd just said.

"My life mate," I choked out. "Well, what do I have to do to find him?"

Jeff smiled, pushing the chart in my direction. "You don't have to do anything. Just go to places where there are people — the kind of people you want to meet."

He made it sound so simple. But nothing about relationships was simple to me. At thirty-eight, I'd never even come close to marrying, thanks to a strange confluence of factors. For one thing, I was terrified of landing in a 1950s-style marriage like my mother's, one where I would be relegated to the "just a housewife" role and expected to defer my own desires to those of husband and children. That fear was reasonable, but what was less so was the way I'd swallowed Hollywood's magical vision of romantic love as presented in the movies of my growing-up years, the ones in which the feisty girl—Carol Lynley in *Light in the Forest*, Carroll Baker in *How the West Was Won*, Doris Day in *Pillow Talk*—garners the attention of a romantic, slightly dangerous outsider, who promptly gives up his wandering ways to settle down with her. That unrealistic notion led me to spurn solid, caring men in favor of dashing rebels who injected excitement into my life but in the end gave up nothing for me— especially not their freedom.

By the time I graduated from college in 1969, the fantasy Hollywood was peddling had changed slightly. Now we had movie heroines like Katharine Ross in *Butch Cassidy and the Sundance Kid* and Barbra Streisand in *Funny Girl*, heroines who were still feisty, but who were ever-patient and loving no matter what the men in their lives did (Streisand even sang about how her man had other girls, but she loved him anyway). These heroines embarked on sexual relationships with no promise of commitment, and they didn't end up with the man in the end. As a feminist, the imbalance in what was given and received in relationships, 1970s style, galled me, but at the same time I didn't want to be accused of being a man hater, a ball breaker, a bitch. So I went along, putting up with last-minute, offhand invitations, flake-outs after plans were made and reminders to hang loose—all so as not to be accused of being "uptight."

Given all that, it is perhaps not surprising that I had a four-year-old son whose father had chosen not to be a part of his life—and that was only the worst of my bad experiences in relationships. I was so weary of it all, so discouraged. Love just seemed impossible for a nontraditional woman like me—something I would forever seek but never find.

Still, I couldn't quite give up, couldn't suppress my longing for a partner. I wanted to walk into a party holding hands with my husband; I wanted a regular sex life; I wanted a father for my son. I thought of Patrick, the most recent man I had dated. "You want to get married and I think you should," he'd said the last time we were together, "but I'm not the right one. I just finished raising my daughters as a single parent, and I don't want to start over with a young kid. It isn't fair to keep going out with you when I can't give you what you want."

How novel. He was the rare man to be honest about his intentions, to put my needs ahead of his own. I came home and wept that night, in despair over yet another failed relationship, but woke up the next morning feeling like a spell had been broken. I said to myself, *I'm tired of all the trauma and drama. I want a man who wants what I want.* It was then that I had decided to consult Jeff again, hoping he would have some magical insight to help me find lasting love.

But I never expected anything like what he had said to me. Afterward, I went home and found the Experimental College catalog, recalling a class I'd seen in it earlier: "Finding the Relationship You Want." Experimental College classes were offbeat, non-credit, and inexpensive, and they did seem to attract an educated, middle-class crowd. In the past I'd taken classes on everything from writing to dance, facial massage to meditation. I looked again at the class description, which promised that students would learn how to attract the right person into their lives, and thought to myself, *Well, any man who signs up for this class has got to be looking.* I sent off the registration before I had a chance to change my mind.

The class started on a Friday evening in the rented basement room of a church. I slipped into one of the folding chairs that had been set up in the crowded space and looked around. Maybe fifty people, most in their thirties and forties, I guessed. The instructor — a slight, balding, and not very attractive man whom I immediately pegged as an aging hippie — started off by asking us to introduce ourselves to the people close by; I felt a frisson of excitement, wondering if any of them could be the life mate Jeff had talked about. But none of these brief exchanges made an impression on me, and afterward, the teacher launched into a talk that lasted all evening. I almost fell asleep.

The next day's class wasn't much better. I had hoped that we would be divided up into small groups where we would get a chance to become acquainted, but that didn't happen. The instructor simply talked as he had the night before, describing New Age techniques: affirmations, check; visualizations, check; treasure maps, check—all the things I'd already done. He invited questions and comments, but

I didn't feel interested enough to speak. I began to despair of meeting a pleasant man to date, let alone a life mate.

Then, after a lunch break, the students congregated in the parking lot and I found myself in conversation with a small group of people, among them a man who caught my eye. It wasn't because he was good looking. Although he had startling, intensely blue eyes that peeked out beneath bushy brows, he had a very strange nose — with a bump on its bridge and a point at its end — that was too large for his face. His abundant hair was mostly gray, curling over his collar and ending in longish sideburns that reminded me of Neil Diamond at the height of his 1970s fame. But he had an aura of gentleness and warmth that was very appealing. Though he said little, I found myself thinking, *That man has the nicest vibes coming off of him.*

So I talked to the group but my gaze kept coming back to him, watching for his reaction when I spoke. I was going through the motions of conversation, while he just stood there with an enigmatic half-smile on his face that didn't betray his emotions. Yet I was drawn to him. So when it was time to return to the class, I deliberately fell in beside him, Jeff's words ringing in my ears. I knew I had to say something or I might never see him again.

"My intuition tells me I'd like to get to know you," I blurted out, hardly believing my own courage—or perhaps foolhardiness. I braced myself for a cool reception.

But to my relief he nodded. "Yeah, I feel the same way. My name's Maurice."

"I'm Nancy," I said, daring to look a little closer and noticing that he had about two inches on me and clearly worked out regularly. I tamped down the trembling that realization evoked and forged ahead with the practical. "Let's trade phone numbers." We stopped in the hallway and I fumbled in my purse for paper and pen while Maurice waited patiently, that same half smile on his face.

I came home feeling hopeful, but my good spirits quickly gave way to worry as I remembered how forward I'd been with him. Did Maurice feel threatened? Did he only give me his number to placate me? I was relieved and excited when he called me two days later.

"I wondered if we might spend Saturday afternoon together," he said after the hellos and how-are-yous.

I hesitated—I hadn't told him that I had a son. "Um, how do you feel about kids?" I thought about the personal ads that described having children as being "encumbered," and about the men I'd met who had retreated as soon as they got that information.

But his voice was as warm as the aura he'd given off when I met him. "I think they're fine. Why? Do you have some?"

"One — a four-year-old boy."

"Well, maybe we could do something that includes him. We could go to the zoo."

I let out the breath I'd been holding. "He loves the zoo, and it's only a few blocks from my house . . . Oh, wait, I just remembered, I'm babysitting my friend's son."

"Then we'll take both of them."

And we did. At the zoo, Maurice knelt down to talk to the boys on their level, giggling along with them when they acted silly. I took a photo of the trio as they stood together, Maurice's square hands on my son's shoulders. They looked like father and son.

By evening it was clear we weren't done, so I got a babysitter and Maurice and I went to a movie, *Murphy's Romance*. It featured Sally Field as a weary single mother finding love with a nice-guy older man (James Garner) after years of dealing with a ne'er-do-well ex-husband. The parallels weren't lost on me, though the age gap between Maurice and me was only five years, not twenty.

Afterward, we went to a pub, a dark wood-paneled college hangout featuring high-backed booths with candles on the tables. We gazed at each other over nachos and Chardonnay, both of us a bit dazed by the sudden intimacy of our day together.

"I was married before, for eighteen years," Maurice told me, taking a sip of wine. "I have a sixteen-year-old daughter—she lives with her mom. I don't get to see her as often as I'd like." He looked across the room at a rowdy table for six, where a drinking game seemed to be underway. I looked too, smiling as I thought of my own college days.

"How long have you been divorced?" I asked with some trepidation, having learned through experience that newly-divorced men tended to be too fragile and gun shy to make good partners.

"Almost five years."

That was a relief. "Your choice or hers?" I pulled a chip from our basket of nachos.

Maurice chuckled. "You really go for the jugular, don't you?" He was silent for a moment, but didn't seem offended by my inquisitiveness—rather searching for the right words. "Well, it was my choice, but really, we'd been growing apart for a while. She remarried less than a year after the divorce."

"And you?"

He shrugged. "I've had some relationships—nothing serious." He studied me for a minute. "What happened with your son's father?"

I took a big swallow of wine and sighed. The moment of truth. "We were living together, but he left when I told him I was pregnant, said he didn't want the responsibility. I thought long and hard before deciding to go through with having the baby."

"That must have been difficult for you." His voice was kind; I didn't hear any disapproval of my being an "unwed mother."

"It was. It is. But it's worth it."

Maurice looked at me with what I took to be tenderness. "I admire you," he said.

By the time the day was over, I was convinced that Maurice was as much the solid nice guy as James Garner had been on the screen. I came home that night feeling so high that I could barely sleep, yet at the same time strangely peaceful.

Two weeks later I told a friend, "I think I've met the man I'm going to marry." And then I sucked in my breath, surprised at my own words. *Usually I hedge my bets, say something like 'Well, he seems nice. We'll see.' But this time I seem to be sure.*

As it turned out, I was right. Maurice and I were a couple from the moment we met, and eighteen months later we married.

I've told this story many times, as new people in our lives have asked, "How did you two meet?" But over the years my presentation of it has changed. At first I gushed, "Jeff's prediction was just uncanny. He called himself an astrologer, but I think he was a psychic." Then, over time, I began to wonder if he really was as sure as he had sounded. I'd laugh and say, "Well, maybe he just said what he said to give me courage—and it worked!" Still later, I asked myself why I'd gone to Jeff in the first place. What was it I sought from him and all the other "magicians" I consulted? The answer is something I was loath to admit in my tale telling: I wanted certainty. I wanted someone to tell me what would happen so that I could act to make it come true.

Now, more than thirty years after meeting my husband, I believe that there is no certainty in this world, but real magic happens when I take action without it, led by the truths I hold in my heart. For a long time I believed that someone like me would have difficulty finding love, that I had to prove myself worthy by being so special that an elusive outsider would change his stripes for me. I had to learn to trust what my heart had always known—that I was lovable, just as I was. Jeff knew that, not because he was a psychic, but because it's true of everyone. He sowed the seeds of magic; only I could make love bloom.

Contributors' Notes

T.D. Allen By day T.D. Allen is a technical writer and by night a short story writer/ aspiring novelist. A Virginia native, T.D. Allen has lived abroad in Berlin, London and Sydney, places that inspire much of her writing. She holds degrees from Duke University (B.A.) and George Mason University (M.F.A. in Creative Writing).

Ronda Beaman Dr. Ronda Beaman is the Chief Creative Officer for PEAK Learning, Inc., a Clinical Professor of Leadership at The Orfalea School of Business, California Polytechnic University, the Founder and Executive Director of the non-profit Dream Makers SLO, and serves on the Board of Directors for the National Pay It Forward Foundation. Her national award-winning book, *You're Only Young Twice*, has been printed in five languages. Her memoir, *Little Miss Merit Badge* was an Amazon bestseller and was featured at The Golden Globe Awards. Her new book, *Seal With a Kiss*, is designed to improve skills for beginning readers and is offered at Lindamood-Bell Learning Centers internationally.

Cathy Cruise Cathy Cruise's first novel, *A Hundred Weddings,* was published in December 2016 by Possibilities Publishing. Her short stories have appeared in journals such as *American Fiction, Blue Mesa Review, New Virginia Review, Phoebe*, and *Michigan Quarterly Review.* She has a BA in English from Radford University and an MFA in creative writing from George Mason University. She works as an editor in Northern Virginia and is currently writing her second novel.

Barbara Meri Frey Barbra Meri Frey grew up in Brooklyn, New York. She received her BA in English from SUNY-Binghamton in Binghamton, New York. She worked various jobs in publishing and public relations before receiving her MFA in creative writing from George Mason University in Fairfax, Virginia where her innovative style and polished prose distinguished her. Her creative work was published in *Pipe Dream, SPIN*, and *New Virginia Review.* Barbra died in 1994 at age 27.

Karen Guzman Karen Guzman's debut novel *Homing Instincts*, was published in 2014 by Fiction Attic Press. Her short story collection, *Pilgrims and Other Stories*, was a finalist for the St. Lawrence Book Award, and she has published short fiction in a number of literary magazines. She is currently at work on a new novel.

Jenna R. London Jenna R. London earned her MFA from Vermont College of Fine Arts in 2017. Her work has been published in *Assay: A Journal of Nonfiction*

Studies, E the Environmental Magazine, Wildflower Muse, and elsewhere. She is an editor and freelance writer at work on her first essay collection. She lives in upstate New York.

William Lychack William Lychack is the author of a novel, *The Wasp Eater,* a collection of stories, *The Architect of Flowers,* and a forthcoming novel, *Cargill Falls.* His work has appeared in *The Best American Short Stories, The Pushcart Prize,* and on public radio's *This American Life,* and he currently teaches at the University of Pittsburgh.

James Magner, MD James Magner, M.D. is a physician (endocrinologist) and scientist who has studied the biochemistry and physiology of thyroid-stimulating hormone (TSH). Jim was raised in a small town, Quincy, Illinois, which was full of hardworking, thrifty, down-to-earth people just like the characters in his story, *Crazy Aunt Ruth's Legacy.* The story is fiction, but Jim's actual Great Aunt Ruth really did send a Bible salesman running a day after her husband Jack's obituary appeared in the newspaper. His award winning story, *The Message,* appeared in in *2 Elizabeths' Love and Romance Anthology* (2018), and his humorous memoir, *Free to Decide: Building a Life in Science and Medicine* (2015), is being used by students at two universities. Jim plans for a collection of short stories to appear in 2019.

Bill Mesce, Jr Bill Mesce, Jr. is an adjunct instructor on several college campuses in his native New Jersey. He is an occasional writer, screenwriter, and playwright.

Colleen Kearney Rich Colleen Kearney Rich is the author of the chapbook *Things You Won't Tell Your Therapist,* forthcoming in January 2019 from Finishing Line Press. One of the founding editors of *So to Speak: A Feminist Journal of Literature and Art,* she is currently a fiction editor at *Literary Mama.* Her writing has been published in *Wigleaf, Jellyfish Review, matchbook, Minerva Rising, SmokeLong Quarterly,* and *Harpoon Review.* She lives in Virginia.

Nancy Wick Nancy Wick worked for many years as a writer and editor at the University of Washington in Seattle; during that time she won numerous regional and national writing awards from the Council for the Advancement and Support of Education. Now retired, she writes personal essays and other nonfiction and has also worked as a developmental editor. Her work has appeared in *Minerva Rising, Persimmon Tree, Oasis Journal,* and *Longridge Review,* among others.

Acknowledgements

Above all else, I must acknowledge, and thank *everyone* who submitted to this anthology. Each year the quality of submissions improves which then makes our job of choosing the winning selections that much harder. But it is a good problem to have, so I'm not complaining, even though every rejection was a tiny stab to our hearts.

Words cannot properly express my gratitude to this year's judges Cathy Cruise and Jennifer Crawford. Especially to Cathy Cruise who went above and beyond the roll of the a judge to be a sounding board, and a wonderful voice in my ear to keep me on schedule and focused.

A *gigantic* thank you to my amazingly patient and talented cover designer Tim Ford who once again worked within an incredibly tight deadline to put together the cover for this anthology. Without his patience and talent this anthology would be coverless and cold.

And I can't do an acknolwedgement section without a shout-out to my author and friend PJ Devlin, who said to me five years ago "you should start an annual anthology contest!" Despite all of the times when I'm racing against a deadline or chasing down contributor bios and cursing this project, at the end of the day, I am always grateful to have undertaken the challenge.